The Gospel and Mother Goose

Donald E. Miller

Illustrations by Lisa Miller

BRETHREN PRESS

Elgin, Illinois

The Gospel and Mother Goose

BRETHREN PRESS, 1451 Dundee Avenue,
Elgin, IL 60120

Cover design by Kathy Kline
Art by Lisa Miller

Library of Congress Cataloging-in-Publication Data

Miller, Donald Eugene.
The Gospel and Mother Goose.

Bibliography: p.
1. Children's literature—History and criticism.
2. Christianity and literature. I. Title.
PN1009.5.C45M54 1987 809'.89282 87-5180
ISBN 0-87178-320-7
Manufactured in the United States of America

Contents

·1·

The Story's the Thing

In the beginning was the Word, and the Word was with God, and the Word was God. He was in the beginning with God; all things were made through him, and without him was not anything made that was made.

—John 1:1–3

Once upon a time there were no stories for children. For that matter there were no stories for anyone. People did not laugh because there were no stories to laugh at. People did not understand one another because there were no stories to understand. People did not form communities because there were no stories to hold them together. And people were afraid of the world around them because there were no stories by which to relate to it. So God looked upon the people and was moved, because God was a great storyteller. Therefore God put stories in the hearts of people, and the people began to tell stories to one another. People then began to laugh and to understand one another. They began to form communities and to become curious about their world. But best of all, there were stories for children.

The message of this book is simple: storytellers control the age in which they live and give us significant images of ourselves, our communities, our world, and our history. Human beings are inveterate storytellers, for stories are closely related to what we understand to be real. In the words of the opening paragraph, God gave us stories because God is a storyteller.

The pages that follow consider stories for children. Now the number of stories for children is staggering and grows continually. One must therefore be selective. The chapters of this book offer a discussion of a few representative classical children's stories as well as several contemporary children's stories. Simply stated, my purpose is to carry out a dialogue between the meaning of these stories and the meaning of the Christian faith. This approach presumes that children's stories are meaningful and that they have some kind of relationship to the Christian faith. These are rather large presumptions, needing at least some kind of explanation.

How can one find the meaning of a story? Consider for example the well known story of the Gingerbread Man. Is it not merely a story about a cookie that runs away from the little old woman and the little old man who made it, as well as from the horse, the cow, and the other animals it meets along the way? Is is not merely a story that delights three- or four-year-old children? Of course the story is all of that, but still one can inquire further into its meaning. While we can be quite sure that a three- or four-year-old is not interested in the "meaning" of this or any other story, nevertheless, *adults* who tell such stories to children can ask *themselves* about the meaning of the story. To do so is to hear the story both as an adult and as a child, something that an adult can hardly avoid doing.

This inquiry is more than an exercise in curiosity, although that in itself might be sufficient. Adults are constantly interested in what kinds of stories to read to children and what effects these stories have upon them. In fact, many stories for children through the years have been told to them in order to have a particular effect, usually to encourage the adoption of certain moral values. Much children's literature has an obvious socialization function.

There is a clear hint in the story of the Gingerbread Man that a child who runs away from home will get into bad trouble. Inevitably the child will identify with the gingerbread man simply because the gingerbread man's character is the theme and main subject of the story. One thinks of the urge

The Gingerbread Man

for independence in two- and three-year-old children, as well as older children. The two- or three-year-old is quite likely to run away, expecting the parent to give chase. While a parent at a grocery store may find the game more than he or she wants, the child clearly gets great delight from it. So the child's need for independence is reflected in the gingerbread man, whose challenge to everyone is the repeated chant of the story: "Run, run, run as fast as you can. You can't catch me; I'm the Gingerbread Man."

The loneliness of the little old man and the little old woman who first baked the cookie for companionship may go unnoticed by a child, but every adult knows the meaning of that experience. The theme of eating is also in the story. One can hardly miss it since the story is about a cookie that was baked and, finally, eaten. "But then gingerbread men are meant to be eaten." Eating is to a small child as sex is to an adult. Every child knows the fascination of eating and the fantasy of being eaten. Parents can always bring delight to a small child by pretending to by a wild animal and threatening, "I'll eat you up." So the story seems to touch upon a number of psychological themes.

The Gingerbread Man is probably a folktale rather than a fable, myth, an epic, or a modern fantasy story. It seems to have arisen from much retelling and therefore could be expected to have several versions. We are not surprised to find that the Scandanavian story of "The Pancake" has the same structure and theme as "The Gingerbread Man." The pancake jumps out of a pan to escape a hungry family consisting of mother, father, and seven children. Like the gingerbread man, the rolling pancake meets a series of animals and becomes more insulting to each one.

"Good day, pancake," said the gander.

"The same to you, Gander Pander," said the pancake.

"Pancake, dear, don't roll so fast; bide a bit and let me eat you up."

"When I have given the slip to Goody Poody, and the good man, and seven squalling children, and Manny Panny, and Henny Penny, and Cocky Locky, and Ducky Lucky, and Goosey Poosey, I may well slip through your feet, Gander

Pander," said the pancake, which rolled off as fast as ever.

So when it had rolled a long, long time, it met a pig.

"Good day, pancake," said the pig.

"The same to you, Piggy Wiggy," said the pancake, which without a word more, began to roll and roll like mad."[1] The frenzied rolling is useless, for the fated pancake is soon gobbled up by the pig, just as the gingerbread man is soon swallowed by the fox.

The setting is in rural life of a previous era with geese, cows, and ducks along the road. It is about persons and animals for whom eating is a concern and for whom poverty seems to be a constant threat. The story likely functions to keep independence from turning to insolence in the community.

"Good day, pancake," said the pig.

We have noticed the sheer delight of the story, with its alliterative phrases, regularly repeated; "Run, run, run as fast as you can." The play with words appeals to the very young, for they are learning to play with words in an initial stage of finding out what words mean. We have noticed the moral teaching of the story in its gentle criticism of exaggerated independence, insolence, and arrogance. The psychological elements of eating, individuality, and loneliness have been noted. We have also recognized the story in its setting as folktale. Have we exhausted its meaning?

What about plot development? In form the account is a chase story with a cumulative plot. Each encounter allows a repetition of what was said before. The story begins with an act of arrogance, a challenge to the little old man and the little old woman. The primary repeated theme, "You can't catch me," contains a self-deception that becomes clear as the story progresses. The half hidden truth is that no one can outrun everyone and everything. The story develops as a series of encounters in which the deception becomes more and more plausible, at least for a time.

Resolution comes with the meeting of the fox, (or the pig). The river is the inevitable limit to all aspiration, the limit which the assertion "You can't catch me," has ignored. There is no alternative but to trust the fox, the least trustworthy of all the characters, in order to cross. Dramatically the fox forces the gingerbread man to move up to the fox's head, for the unfortunate cookie has no other choice. Finally, of course, the fox gulps him down. Now the self-deception of the original boast becomes clear. No one is independent enough to be without limits. No one can outrun everyone and everything.

This story, like so many children's stories, may be found in a number of variations. We have already noted "The Pancake," which is also something entitled "Johnnycake Ho." Even the account of the gingerbread man has variations. A major variation takes away the fox at the end. One recent version suggests that the gingerbread man is still enjoying himself as he runs. Such an ending changes the whole structure of the story. Running is no longer a self-deception, for the limit on aspiration is taken away.

The editor may have considered the story to be discouraging to children, or perhaps the changed story more nearly reflects the incessant running which is a symbol of the American way of life. Novels like John Updike's *Rabbit, Run* contain the same theme that depicts life as a constant running. It is possible that the editor wanted to take the violence out of the story. In any case the structure and the total point of view is considerably different with the alternate ending.

Is the meaning of the story now exhausted? Not at all. Likely the reader will find in the story a meaning not mentioned here. The point is not to exhaust the meaning but rather to begin to open the significance of a story that may otherwise be obscure. There is more than one way to interpret a story. It is open to multiple interpretations. However, every interpretation should take account of such structural elements as theme, plot, setting, character, point of view, and style. Along with the structures of the story one may consider morality, psychological functions, human development, social setting, and the history of the telling of the story—all of which we have illustrated with the story of the Gingerbread Man. Without some discipline of interpretation any statement about the story is equally plausible.

Finally, the story has its own existential meaning, its own beauty. Unless the story is delightful in itself, no consideration of it is worth the effort. Furthermore, the reflection is simply a way of enriching the story or of considering if and how it will be told. Such consideration can never substitute for the story itself. The reader should not ignore this assertion. It would be pointless in telling the story to substitute any reflection made about the gingerbread man for any part of the story itself.

I introduced this discussion by indicating that its purpose is to carry out a dialogue between the meaning of selected children's stories and the meaning of the Christian faith. We have now given an example of how to find meaning in a representative classical children's story. How then does the view of reality in the gingerbread man compare with the view of reality in the Christian faith? Here again this opens a very large question, for many people differ regarding the meaning of the Christian faith.

Inevitably my own view of the Christian faith will be given, a view that is informed by such writers as Karl Barth, Paul Tillich, Dietrich Bonhoeffer, Ernst Troeltsch, Menno Simons, Martin Luther, and John Calvin, to mention only a few. The reader will also see in these pages regular references to the Bible, the essential element in such dialogue. It is possible that my own Church of the Brethren allegiance will be obvious, although there is no intent to remind the reader of it.

Theology today is recovering the concept of story. There may be many reasons, but one is that there is a growing effort to conceptualize continuing change in the Christian understanding of faith while at the same time keeping the continuity of what has gone before. Theologians are therefore working with concepts like history and process to replace the idea of eternally fixed truths. Such efforts are not necessarily a denial of the eternal character of God, but, at the very least, they do affirm that human understanding of God is constantly changing. The only understanding we have is our understanding. In effect then, God's relationship to us seems to be changing within history. So we must reach for the continuity, yet acknowledge the reality of change. Perhaps such a development was inevitable because of the view of history that developed in ancient Israel and was intensified in the New Testament. It was an understanding that history changed, and moved toward a divine goal. The Bible itself is an ongoing story, so is the life of the church, and so is the life of all humanity.

Within the larger story contained in the Bible there are many smaller examples of story. The Bible is full of stories in the form of folktales, sagas, biographies, short stories, parables, histories, and accounts of the "last days." The gospel itself is a story form. The concept of story, therefore, has many dimensions to it, and may be an expecially appropriate form in which to interpret the fuller meaning of the gospel.

The story of the gospel is the story of God with us in Jesus Christ, of the new reign of God, which is a reign of love, peace, and justice for all people. The story of the gospel is a story of God's forgiveness of those who believe, of God's providence in creating and sustaining life, of a community of persons who hope to embody Christ's love to all people. The story of the gospel is the story of the transformation of humanity in the face of constant perversity. It is the story of one person who was able to accept the consequences of that perversity while representing God's love. The gospel is the story of the birth of a new and powerful hope in human life. In the gospel one tastes the overcoming of the fear of death and the conquering of the reigning power of human selfishness. The gospel is a glimpse of that time in which all things in heaven and on earth will be subject to the love of God in Jesus Christ.

In the Bible there are chase stories somewhat reminiscent of the gingerbread man. A good example is the story of Jonah. When asked to preach to the Ninevites, Jonah attempted to flee as far as he could from his Maker. He reached the limit of his race in the water, in a fish rather than a fox. The result, however, was the same: the gingerbread man and Jonah were swallowed. But for Jonah the story is not over. Cast up again, he decided to obey God's command, with the result that the Ninevites repented. The story of Jonah is a story of change in the face of the threat of destruction.

But even more fundamental in the biblical account is that humanity rebelled against their Maker deceiving themselves into thinking that they were more powerful than God. The Calvinist understanding of the theme, with its emphasis on salvation of the elect, is best known. Humanity, made of dust, turns against the Maker in an enormous self-deception and then continues to exercise individual aspiration within an underlying illusion of omnipotence. The technical word for the desire to replace God is *hybris*. Death itself will break that illusion for every person. From dust we came and to dust we will return. However, for those whom God has chosen, the penalty of their self-deception is taken on by God himself in the person of Jesus Christ. God saves the chosen ones from the full force of their self-deception and the threat and power of dying is overcome.

The story of the gingerbread man is the story of aspiration without limitation, and in that sense is like the Calvinist account of humanity running from God. The story is parallel to one theme in the gospel story, but omits the redemption theme. Perhaps one should not expect too much from one story. When the story is changed to eliminate the fox, it becomes a story of humanity's playful running. Certainly running is often enjoyable; however, the resulting story loses much depth. Were the story to suggest that running is the fate of humankind, then it would be more true to our time, for the element of self-deception would be regained.

In very significant ways the story of the gingerbread man parallels the gospel story, but in other ways it does not. The story in most of its forms does teach young children to recognize the feeling of self-delusion. Children may not understand it in this way, certainly not as an idea like "aspiration without limitation," suggested earlier. Still something of that meaning is in the structure of the story, unless it is changed in the storytelling situation.

Perhaps the method of this book is now more clear. I am setting out to interpret a number of classical and modern children's stories, and then to compare these interpretations with the gospel story. While it may be presumptuous to interpret children's stories in such a fashion, it is inevitably done whenever we make decisions about which stories to tell. Hopefully my interpretations are done with a certain critical awareness of my own religious values. The ultimate aim is that the stories be told more often rather than that they be changed. Contemporary storytelling has been transformed by production and market values. Television has practically taken over storytelling. This work is meant to be an encouragement of telling stories in an intimate setting as a way of participating more deeply in giving life meaning.

Within this method the story as interpreted will be compared to the gospel. The comparison takes place as a reflection from both sides in order to find common themes and differences. There will always be some ways in which the story is like the gospel account and other ways in which it is different. Identifying the similarities and the differences is the heart of this approach. My hope is that both the children's story and our understanding of the gospel thereby will be enriched. I do not advocate preaching to children, necessarily, nor the telling of secular stories in the church, although inevitably both such procedures may flow from what is done here in spite of my caution. The ultimate goal of this book, rather, is to deepen the sense of the power of the story, to encourage storytelling in intimate settings, and to enlarge our ability to evaluate critically the stories we tell children.

Other approaches to children's stories are often more structured. Some would want to change the Mother Goose rhymes so that they become a clear advocate of prayer and being good.[2] The result in my judgment is a legalism that can actually inhibit the moral sensitivity and growth of children. Is not the gospel a liberation from such legalism? Others will inevitably want to decide that a given story clearly proclaims the gospel and another story does not. My method is given more to finding analogies between stories and less to approval or disapproval of a story. The stories to be considered have already proven themselves by the fact that many, many children enjoy hearing them told. Some storytellers want to eliminate violence from all stories. My method does not resolve that issue quickly. Rather we set out together to suggest what the story might mean as told, and then to compare that to the gospel. Having made such a comparison we are in a much better position to consider what a given story says about the meaning of violence.

My approach in this discussion attempts to be dialogical, as Paul Tillich used the term. He considered that all culture is religious in its depths. Culture is the form of religion and religion is the depth of culture. This is as true of children's stories as of any other part of human culture. The hope, then, is to find the religious depth of representative children's stories. To this end the following chapters will focus on stories in the collections of Mother Goose, the Grimm brothers, Hans Christian Andersen, Lewis Carroll, Robert Louis Stevenson, Frank Baum, C. S. Lewis, A. A. Milne, and a number of others. May the reader enjoy reading about these as much as I enjoy discussing them.

Notes

1. "Tales from the Fjeld," quoted in Zena Sutherland and May Hill Arbuthnot, *Children and Books,* (Glenview, IL: Scott Foresman, 1977), p. 147.
2. See for example Marjorie Ainsborough Decker, *The Christian Mother Goose Treasury*, (Grand Junction, CO: C. M. G. Productions, Inc., 1980). Decker's alterations are often cleverly done.

·2·

Mother Goose's Melodies

Old Mother Goose,
When she wanted to wander,
Would ride through the air
On a very fine gander.[1]

In view of the great wealth of contemporary children's books, it is hard to realize that modern literature for children is only about three centuries old. Prior to the printing of *Contes de ma Mere l'Oye (Tales of Mother Goose)* by Charles Perrault about 1697, very few printed stories were available for children.[2]

One can imagine that children have always listened to the stories of their grandparents or other storytellers. Surely children since time immemorial have overheard stories of adults which were really not intended for young ears. The great community celebrations of all people have included vivid stories and songs that children could understand. Yet books of stories intended for children are of very recent origin.

During the Middle Ages Latin primers, hand printed by monastic scribes, were available to the children of the wealthy. In the eleventh century Anselm of Canterbury wrote a handbook of manners, morals, science, and religious precepts for the instruction of children, but the book was intended for adults.[3] In the late fifteenth century, William Caxton, England's first printer, produced a book of Aesop's fables. The tales are said to have originated from a Greek slave in the sixth century B.C. They were translated to Latin and became a standard textbook in medieval schools. Though

Caxton probably intended his book of fables for adults, it quickly became popular with children.

Hornbooks and chapbooks in the sixteenth to the eighteenth centuries were precursors to the comic books and children's TV of today. Hornbooks consisted of a wooden paddle with a parchment covered with a translucent piece of horn, and were very durable. Chapbooks were little books of adventure stories sold by peddlers to children for a few pennies.

The Moravian educator, John Amos Comenius (1592-1671), prepared what is generally considered to be the first picture book for children.[4] Soon after that John Bunyan wrote *Pilgrim's Progress*, a story that was much influenced by his reading of chapbooks as a youth. Bunyan's book was not written for children. When the longer theological sections were left out, however, the story became popular with children.

Against this historical background Perrault's *Tales of Mother Goose* were a dramatic leap. A great delight to children, the book established the importance of making such stories available to children. Perrault's stories were these: "The Sleeping Beauty," "Little Red Riding Hood," "Blue Bear," "Puss in Boots," "Diamonds and Toads," "Cinderella," and "Little Thumb," most of which continue to be loved by children today. In place of the longstanding practice of moralizing to children, Perrault's Mother Goose simply delighted them.

Mother Goose crossed the English channel about 1781 or, perhaps, earlier when the John Newbery family published an edition of *Mother Goose's Melodies* or *Sonnets for the Cradle*. The 1781 edition of *Mother Goose's Melodies* was published by T. Carnan, Newbery's stepson, and it may have been the original edition. Newbery (or Carnan) did not simply reproduce Perrault's six stories, but, rather, he included a whole set of delightful poetry for young children.

Mother Goose came to America about 1785 in what is thought to be a pirated reprint of an early Newbery edition.[5] Later editions printed between 1823 and 1833 by the firm, Munroe and Francis of Boston, claimed to be "The Only True

Mother Goose Melodies." The various editions are the framework for contemporary collections of Mother Goose stories. Publishing claims as to the true Mother Goose must be set within this story.

Newbery's strong influence upon the Mother Goose rhymes reflect eighteenth century British life and tradition. However the task of finding deeper meaning in the verse is filled with difficulty. There are many suggestions about how a poem may be related to a historical event or a particular person. Often there is no strong historical reason to accept such suggestions.

In *The Oxford Dictionary of Nursery Rhymes*, Iona and Peter Opie criticize efforts at interpretation:

> Much ingenuity has been exercised to show that certain nursery rhymes have had greater significance than is now apparent. They have been vested with mystic symbolism, linked with social and political events, and numerous attempts have been made to identify the nursery characters with real persons. It should be stated straightaway that the bulk of these speculations are worthless. Fortunately the theories are so numerous they tend to cancel each other out.[6]

In spite of such caution let us look at the meaning of the rhymes. It would be foolish to claim to know certainly what a rhyme means or to be sure that it is related to a particular event. Yet being more than nonsense syllables, they are open to interpretation.

There are many stories, pranks, finger-plays, toe-plays, games, riddles, counting rhymes, proverbs, superstitions, calendar verses, dialogues, songs, tongue twisters, cumulative stories, odd situations, grotesque accounts, and nonsense rhymes in the Mother Goose collections.

Consider the prank:

Georgie Porgie, pudding and pie,
Kissed the girls and made them cry.
When the boys came out to play.
Georgie Porgie ran away.

The alliteration and careful rhyming are delightful, no matter what the words say. The cadence and rhythm can catch an infant's fancy regardless of meaning. However, the words make obvious reference to gender roles. One gets the sense that Georgie Porgie has difficulty relating to both girls and boys.

An earlier version was as follows:

Rowley Powley, pudding and pie,
Kissed the girls and made them cry;
When the girls began to cry,
Rowley Powley runs away.[7]

This earlier version makes better sense of the phrase "pudding and pie," for it suggests a person who is overweight from eating sweets. The focus here is upon a boy teasing girls. A difficulty with boys is not as evident as with Georgie Porgie. At least one person has suggested that Georgie Porgie was George I of England, but there sems to be no way to be sure.[8]

One of the reasons a rhyme of this kind is so appealing is that all children know boys who tease girls, making them cry; and all children know girls who cry easily upon being teased.

Georgie Porgie illustrates an objection that may be brought against the Mother Goose rhymes. They tend to reflect gender stereotyping of a previous era. The objection is that the three-year-old who learns the verse will be taught that it is normal and acceptable behavior for boys to kiss girls against their wishes. Girls are to be demure, and are to be (or at least appear to be) hurt by aggressive male behavior. The verse teaches traditional gender roles long before children are aware of being taught.

An answer to this objection is that without doubt the many roles of human interaction are deeply embedded in children's verses. Since Mother Goose reflects the life of two centuries ago, it also reflects gender roles and other social roles from that time. Children should hear contemporary rhymes reflecting today's customs. Yet children become impoverished if they are not able to hear and taste the way life was lived in other centuries.

Marriage relationships are reflected in this story:

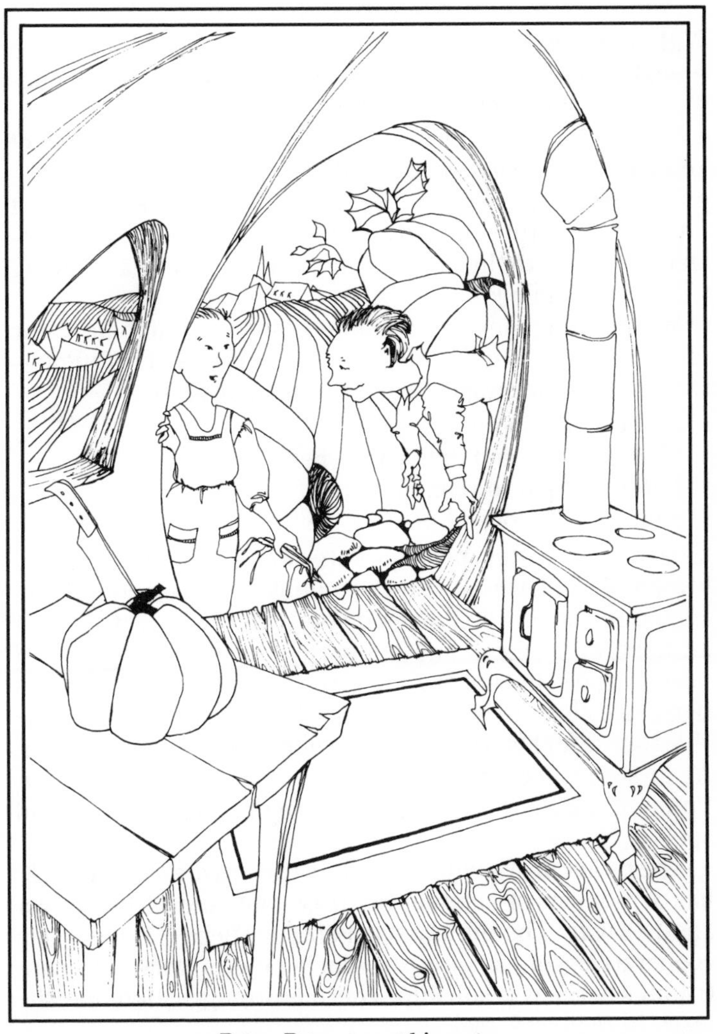

Peter, Peter, pumpkin eater

Peter, Peter, pumpkin eater,
Had a wife and couldn't keep her;
He put her in a pumpkin shell,
And there he kept her very well.

Without knowing the source of this verse the reader would probably agree that the theme of pumpkins and of husband-wife relationship are basic. It would seem that Peter often eats pumpkins, that indeed pumpkins may be the staple of Peter's diet. *Annotated Mother Goose* suggests that pumpkins are, perhaps, the most beloved vegetable of juvenile literature. The reference could be to a jack-o-lantern which, to the imagination, may appear as a dwelling with a person inside.

Where pumpkins are a common food, a pumpkin eater might be one who could afford to eat little else. This suggestion gains some support from the second verse.

Peter, Peter, pumpkin eater,
Had another, and didn't love her!
Peter learned to read and spell,
And then he loved her very well.

Clearly uneducated, perhaps Peter was a poor man reduced to a simple diet. In that case the pumpkin shell could symbolize the shell of poverty around Peter. Peter's wife would not be kept well unless she submitted to the constraints of poverty and consented to live in the pumpkin's shell. Education could change this. An educated man is more likely to be able to care for his wife, and more likely to be able to love her. As in several other Mother Goose rhymes, "Peter, Peter, Pumpkin Eater" encourages children to learn to read and spell.

The problem of gender roles is in this rhyme as well. Peter has a problem of keeping his first wife, and of loving yet another wife. The initiative is Peter's. There is no hint of a cooperative relationship in which Peter's wife also contributes to the relationship. There is no suggestion that she learn to read and spell.

To be kept well by being placed in a shell offends one's sense of mutuality, yet it is the centuries old tradition of marriage. The problem is not so much the limitation, which will always be present, but the fact that total initiative is given to the male role. The New Testament vision is that in God's kingdom there is neither male nor female. Paul's way of putting it is that the husband is to love the wife as himself and be willing to sacrifice all for her; and the woman is to do likewise. Here there is a kind of mutuality of initiative that seems to be missing in the children's verse. Whether or not we have gone too far in interpreting this verse, the problem of mutuality between husband and wife has been very basic through the centuries. Christianity certainly supports education, but the basic problem is relational.

Another popular verse is this:

Little Miss Muffet
Sat on a tuffet,
Eating her curds and whey;
There came a big spider,
Who sat down beside her
And frightened Miss Muffet away.

Little Miss Muffet

A problem for the understanding is that "tuffet" has virtually no meaning. Illustrators have often chosen a stool, a pillow, or a grassy place. Older versions seem to begin, "Little Mary Ester sat on a tester . . .," or "Little Miss Mopsey sat in the shopsey . . .," suggesting that Muffet and tuffet may be a nonsense pair of words. The curds and whey eaten by Miss Muffet is a reference to cheese. The whey is the thinner part of the milk that remains when the other part coagulates. Curds and whey was probably a common food, and so Miss Muffet is undistinguished by where she sits or what she eats.

Stories for children often have animals or creatures that frighten young women. One thinks of the frog that the princess must kiss to gain her prince or the donkey that the princess must love to discover her lover. The theme is that of a young woman being frightened by animal vitality. Sigmund Freud put it most directly when he suggested that such creatures are unconscious reminders of sexual encounter with a male.

Here again we get a picture of female timidity and fear of natural vitality. Certainly women must come to terms with the reality of natural processes. However the same is true of men, for most men are also afraid of snakes and spiders. There is good reason for this fear, for many snakes and spiders are poisonous. This verse like others cited does two things. It recognizes that young women are often afraid of animal vitality, but it also teaches young women to be that way.

Some nursery rhymes may have a particular historical reference:

Mary, Mary, quite contrary,
How does your garden grow?
With silver bells and cockle shells
And pretty maids all in a row.

The reference may be to Mary, Queen of Scots, who had been reared and educated in the Catholic tradition in France. At the time she became heir of the throne in Scotland, the Scottish Reformation was taking place. Nearly all of Scotland followed John Knox in the Scottish Reformed tradition. Mary in remaining loyal to Catholicism, even though she was almost alone in doing so, did seem quite contrary to the people.

The queen lived in Holyrood Castle in Edinburgh where she had her own beautiful grounds and chapel. It was Mary's practice to go through the garden to daily mass accompanied by her women attendants, the pretty maids all in a row. The silver bells may refer to the bells rung during mass, and the cockle shells to the rosary beads. So the picture of Mary, Mary, quite contrary may refer to Mary, Queen of Scots, and her attendants going to mass.

One can hardly discuss Mother Goose without mentioning all the instances of cruelty in the stories. Handley-Taylor of Manchester, England, has suggested that an average collection of 200 nursery rhymes contains the following:

8 allusions to murder (unclassified),
2 cases of choking to death,
1 case of death by devouring,
1 case of cutting a human being in half,
1 case of decapitation,
1 case of death by squeezing,
1 case of death by shriveling,
1 case of death by starvation,
1 case of boiling to death

The list goes on until 100 some instances of cruelty have been cited. His conclusion is that "Expressions of fear, weeping, moans of anguish, biting, pain, and evidence of supreme selfishness may be found in almost every other page." Handley-Taylor was calling for reform when he wrote this in 1952.[9] I would suggest a middle road which would eliminate those verses that seem unduly violent. However life is actually full of violence, and children are not helped by ignoring it.

Secular children's stories are often more interesting than church literature just because the secular may be in closer touch with the reality of life. Hope cannot be felt or described until the pain of life is actually touched. The great richness of the Bible is that it is in touch with the pain and hopelessness of life, but witnesses to a way through. Many, perhaps most, of the children of the world experience the pain of abuse, malnourishment, starvation, lack of care, threat of atomic destruction. Stories that ignore these realities are not helpful to children.

The opposite is also true. Stories that dwell upon cruelty or pain without pointing to a way through are not helpful to children. One must not emphasize the cruelty of another age, but the cruelty of this age must be acknowledged, even by children. Children know the difference between the stories and the love that should surround them. It is much more important that the stories reach what is deeply true and hopeful to the child than that all reference to pain be eliminated.

A recent effort to reform Mother Goose is that of Marjorie Ainsworth Decker. Her *Christian Mother Goose* books contain paraphrases of well-known verses. The poetry is changed to bring out the message of God's love in Christ.

Here is one example:

Ding, dong, bell,
There's gladness in the well!
Who put it in?
God! It's genuine!
Who can get it out?
Anyone who doesn't doubt.
Ding, dong, bell,
There's gladness in the well.

The original poem is quite familiar:

Ding, dong, bell,
Pussy's in the well
Who put her in?
Little Johnny Green.
Who pulled her out?
Little Johnny Stout.
What a naughty boy was that
To try to drown poor pussy cat,
Who never did him any harm,
But killed the mice in his father's barn.[10]

Decker's paraphrases are often quite clever. She manages

to keep the poetic quality of the verse. Hers is a very direct statement of God's grace and salvation. She is doing very much what other collectors have done. They have adapted and created. Children and their parents will decide whether it is a worthy effort.[11]

Notes

1. *Mother Goose,* Pictures by Gyo Fujikawa. (New York: Grosset and Dunlap, 1968), p. 15.
2. Sutherland and Arbuthnot, *Children and Books,* p. 64.
3. Sutherland and Arbuthnot, *Children and Books,* p. 37.
4. Sutherland and Arbuthnot, *Children and Books,* p. 38.
5. Sutherland and Arbuthnot, *Children and Books,* p. 64.
6. p. 27 as quoted in Sutherland and Arbuthnot, *Children and Books,* p. 65.
7. *The Annotated Mother Goose,* ed. William S. Baring-Gould and Cecil Baring-Gould, (New York: Crown Pubs., Inc., 1982), p. 170.
8. *Annotated Mother Goose,* p. 170.
9. *Annotated Mother Goose,* pp. 20-21.
10. *Mother Goose,* p. 17.
11. Decker, *The Christian Mother Goose Treasury.*

·3·

Enchanting Folklore

The duck came swimming towards them and Hansel got on its back and told his sister to sit on his knee. "No," answered Gretel, "it will be too heavy for the duck. It must take us over one after the other."[1]

Commenting about the fairy tales collected by the brothers Jacob and Wilhelm Grimm, the poet W. H. Auden said that these tales are an indispensable foundation of Western culture. Auden then added, "... it is hardly too much to say that these tales rank next to the Bible in importance."[2] The enormous impact of the Grimm brothers' fairy tales can hardly be better stated.

The achievement of the brothers Grimm is all the more surprising when one realizes that they did not set out to produce a collection of popular children's stories. They were philologists who were studying the roots of Teutonic culture. Enormously skilled in linguistics the Grimms set out to trace the roots of the Teutonic language back to a common primitive religion. To do this they began to collect songs, superstition, and commonly told fairy tales, for they believed they would find the vestigial remains of a much older Teutonic tradition.

The Grimms relied heavily upon one particularly talented storyteller, Frau Viehmann. They were also fortunate that Wilhelm's wife, Dortchen Wild, and her five sisters were very familiar with the stories told to children. From such sources they brought together their first set of fairy tales, which appeared in 1812 under the title *Kinder-und Hausmarchen.*[3] The critics took little notice of this volume, but it soon caught the fancy of children around the world.

The special power of folktales is that they touch something very deep in the human psyche. They are able to symbolize fundamental human dilemmas in a charming way, providing a resolution to a seemingly imponderable dilemma. It is done with delightful imagery and with great sensitivity to the feelings of children. Were one to give direct and reasonable answers to these dilemmas, the answers would get trapped by the dilemmas and great resistance would build up. The stories have the ability to pass through the resistance and work in the depths of the imagination. The story therefore has the power to heal, for it touches a brokenness that cannot otherwise be reached. The stories collected by the Brothers Grimm are especially powerful in this regard.

Consider one of the favorite stories of the Brothers Grimm, "Hansel and Gretel." The plot of the story is simple and direct,but the charm and the subtlety of the story is incomparable. Hansel and Gretel are the only children of a simple wood cutter, whose wife is their stepmother. They live an austere existence, and are on the edge of starvation frequently. On one such occasion the stepmother insists that the children must be left to starve, or all four will die. "You may as well plane the boards for our coffins at once."[4] Against the feeble objections of her husband, she forms a plan to leave the children in the forest to starve. The first effort does not succeed, but a second does. The children are left deep in the forest with nothing to eat.

Wandering in desperation they finally happen upon a quaint house made of bread and cake. When they attempt to eat of the house, they discover that they have been trapped by a wicked witch who prepares to eat them. While the oven is being heated, Gretel finds an opportunity to push the witch into it and lock the door. The children escape with the witch's treasure and find their way home. Their stepmother has died in the meantime, and their father greets them fondly. "So their troubles came to an end, and they lived together as happily as possible."[5]

Hansel and Gretel

With such a deceptively simple plot, we may ask what the story does for children. It revolves around several themes. One is the relationship of children to the negative feelings of the mother (or stepmother) in the presence of a weak father. Another theme is that of eating and starvation. Possibly a third theme is that of the relationship between brother and sister.[6]

The theme of eating runs all through the story. The sad situation was brought on in the beginning by a season of starvation. The children are left in the woods to starve. When they are taken into the forest the second time, Hansel leaves a trail of bread crumbs so that he and Gretel can find their way back, but the birds eat the crumbs. The children must come to terms with the reality that all animals must eat to live. The children in their hunger are enticed by a house made of good things to eat and trapped by the witch who prepares to eat them instead. Most of the story deals with hunger and eating.

In an earlier chapter there was a reference to the importance of eating for children. Small children are greatly interested in the biological functions of the body. In the earliest years there is fascination with eating and elimination. Older children gain interest in sexuality. As stated in an earlier chapter, eating is to young children as sex is to adults. Children must learn the limits of eating and elimination, and later the limits of sexuality. They may not eat everything. In fact, they must learn to distinguish what is edible and what is not. They may not eliminate at any time or any place. Youth and adults must learn the proper occasions to express sexual behavior.

Further, children are fascinated by the fact that they eat other animals, that animals eat one another, and that they themselves are edible. The threat, "I'll eat you up," will bring gales of laughter from any young child. Many of the struggles between children and adults come over questions of what to eat and when. Parents often insist that children must eat their food, when in fact nothing is more certain that children will eat. Yet when told to do so, many children refuse to eat. In the extreme instance refusing to eat can lead to anorexia. The relationship to parents in terms of eating is of central importance to every child. Thus the story of Hansel and Gretel treats a most fundamental theme in human life. Incidentally many of the favorite children's stories deal with the theme of eating, for instance, the Gingerbread Man. Many of the classic stories involve an animal being eaten.

Hansel and Gretel are related to a mother (stepmother) whose need to eat is more powerful than her love for her children. She has no difficulty in letting the children starve if it means that she can eat. The situation is carried one step further with the witch, who is, obviously, the mother in disguise.The witch is willing to eat the children to satisfy her own hunger. In the witch the children finally meet the extreme consequences of an unbridled compulsion to eat.

The reader may find the suggestion that the witch is another personality of the mother to be unfounded. The story itself hints at this several times. To awaken the children for their trek into the forest the mother says, "Get up, you lazy bones," which are the same words that the witch uses to awaken Gretel. Another suggestion that witch and stepmother are one and the same is that once the witch has died in the oven, the children come home to find that their mother also has died. The parallels can hardly be coincidental.

The reference to a stepmother is a psychological device. A stepmother has the caring responsibilities of a mother, but without the love of a mother for her children. The stepmother represents times of uncaring impulses that every mother has toward her children. It is a powerful storytelling device, but enormously unfair to all those stepmothers who have given love equal to that of any mother.

What Hansel and Gretel and the reader must learn is that they will become like the witch if they do not control their eating. In the witch they see the picture of an adult who continues to eat with the unrestricted appetite of a young child. They learn that while bread is a necessity of life, we cannot live on bread alone. Intelligence is as important as bread.

This first becomes evident when Hansel leaves a trail of stones in order to find their way back out of the forest. It becomes decisive when Gretel sees the intention of the witch to cook her. Using her intelligence, Gretel is able to trick the witch into coming near the oven, where she pushes her in. Gretel's self-insight saves both of the children. Telling a child that life is more than bread will have little effect, but telling the story of Hansel and Gretel lets the message slip deeply into the emotions of children. It enables children to handle thier own emotions and to respond to the basic impulses of adults.

At the beginning of the story Hansel's intelligence in scattering the stones seems to be the only hope of saving the children. When they are finally enticed by the witch, Hansel is imprisoned in order to be fattened for better eating. The boy cannot overcome the special rage of the woman, though he deceives her for a time by pretending to need yet more food. It is Gretel's intelligence, however, that finally saves them.

As they are leaving the deep forest they come to "a great piece of water." Hansel sees no way across, but Gretel suggests calling the duck. Climbing on the duck's back, Hansel wants Gretel to sit on his knee. She replies that the duck must take them one at a time. It would seem that each child must gain her or his own truth. Gretel has come into her own in the experience with the witch, and the relationship between the boy and girl has become much more nearly equal.

The significance of the duck becomes more evident when one considers the other birds in the story. "Thousands of birds" ate the crumb path that Hansel had left. A beautifully singing snowbird led them to the witch's cottage when they were lost. The duck helped them cross the impassable piece of water, after which "the wood seemed to grow more and more familiar to them." The birds cut off their return home, led them to the candy house, and led them home again. The birds seem to represent that all-knowing spirit that leads us to face our deepest difficulties and then leads us back to the familiar again. In the biblical stories the Spirit of God leads us to face temptation and then leads us back again to where life can be lived "as happily as possible."

The forest represents the depths of human experience wherein human beings wander without knowing where they are. It is the realm of the unconscious. There the children meet the impulsive depths of life, aided by the birds. They find both all they want to eat and the cannibalistic mother. In those depths they discover their own limits, who they are, and how they are really related to one another. They are, therefore, much better able to accept their father's affection and to live life as happily as possible.

During the Middle Ages the forest was the world in which the depths of life were encountered. In the ancient world stories of the struggle between good and evil took place at sea, and now, in the twentieth century, they occur in outer space. The limits of the known world arouse the whole range of human impulses. That limit is symbolized in the story of Hansel and Gretel by the impassable water.

The Bible's most significant starvation story is that of Israel in the wilderness. In Israel's case the people fled from their oppressor. The wilderness is their forest. As Gretel cries, "If only the wild animals in the forest had eaten us, we should at least have died together," so Israel led by Moses feared that they had gone into the wilderness to starve. Like Hansel and Gretel Israel had to learn to govern their impulses and live by God's commandments. Finally they crossed a body of water, the Jordan, to come to a land where they could live "as happily as possible."

In the biblical story God's guidance is much more evident. Hansel and Gretel seem so innocent, and Israel seems so rebellious. Yet the development of the story is strikingly similar. In the New Testament Jesus recapitulates Israel's journey when he is driven by the Spirit into the wilderness where he is tempted to turn stones to bread. As with Hansel and Gretel and Israel, Jesus had to find the limit to his hunger. So "Hansel and Gretel" is a delightful account of facing the most vexing human impulses. It does so by touching us in the depths of our experience.

Rumplestiltskin, another Grimm brothers' story, is about a miller's daughter who is given to the king after her father boasts that she can spin straw into gold. The king threatens to take her life if she cannot complete this task. In her great distress she promises a strange little man to give him her first child if he will help her. Help her he does, quickly spinning the straw to gold. Later when a child was born, the little man comes to claim his reward. The poor queen begs him to relent, which he agrees to do, should she be able to discover his name in three days. All of her efforts to discover his name are to no avail, however, until the queen's messenger overhears the little man say Rumplestiltskin. When the queen discloses the little man's name, he is so enraged that he tears himself in half.

In this story impossible male expectations made a young woman's life intolerable. The father bragged in order to

Rumplestiltskin

elevate himself in the king's eyes, and the king wanted the gold to elevate himself in the eyes of others. The girl was a pawn in this network of male avarice. Under such demands the woman can only become depressed.

The strange little man does not symbolize the father or the king. He could represent all demanding men. As in so many of the Grimm tales, the little man's character is disclosed in the final scene where in sheer rage he tears himself apart. "The devil told you that," he declares, indicating that only the devil knows his name, and that he belongs to the devil.

The story is that of a young woman who makes a pact with the devil to get out of her dilemma. She is controlled by the little man unless she can name him. To know someone's name is to know who she or he is. The search of the kingdom parallels the search within to discover what controls her. Only the proper name can release her from the rage he represents.

A more modern story that deals with the theme of anger is Maurice Sendak's *Where the Wild Things Are.* Sendak demonstrates the same sense of interior realities that is in the Grimm fairy tales. In Sendak's story Max has been acting wildly so his mother sends him to bed without a meal. There he sails across many days and seas to the land of the wild things who threaten to eat him up, but he dances with them until he is king. Finally against their entreaty, Max returns to his room, where he finds a warm meal waiting for him.

Sendak knows how eating is related both to anger and affection. He does not need a forest to get to deeper motives. Rather, Max sails over seas and times, as well, where he gives himself over to the wild things. Like Hansel and Gretel and the miller's daughter, Max discovers that the wild things will consume him if he allows them. When he decides that the feelings belong to him rather than the feelings owning him, he becomes free to leave. It is a fundamental "no" to unending anger. The feelings do not want to release him, but they have no power when Max has come to know himself. Then he is able to return to his room over the water, as did

Hansel and Gretel. There was Max's meal, a sign of his mother's affection. I am sure that they lived "as happily as possible."

Like the Grimm brothers' stories, Sendak's account of Max touches something deep within us all. The story heals in a much more profound way than saying, "Just count to ten and you will get over it." In the depths of our souls we wrestle with evil spirits. Call them feelings of rage or avarice, if you like. These feelings can tear us apart as was Rumplestiltskin. Stories like Sendak's name these spirits. The attempt to give children stories that reflect only happy and joyful feelings deprives children of what they need to deal with life. The Bible is full of stories of struggles, stories that heal wounds to our innermost feelings. The Bible, too, gives us a way to face the inevitable consuming desires of living. W. H. Auden can say, in truth, that the Grimm fairy tales are second only to the Bible as the foundation of modern Western civilization.

Notes

1. Margaret E. Martignoni (ed.), *The Illustrated Treasury of Children's Literature,* (New York: Grosset and Dunlap, 1955), p. 183.
2. Sutherland and Arbuthnot, *Children and Books,* p. 158.
3. Sutherland and Arbuthnot, *Children and Books,* p. 160.
4. Martignoni, *The Illustrated Treasury,* p. 178.
5. Martignoni, *The Illustrated Treasury,* p. 183.
6. Bruno Bettleheim, *The Uses of Enchantment, The Meaning and Importance of Fairy Tales,* (New York: Vintage Books, 1977) pp. 15-16, lists seven similar sets of themes.

·4·

Fanciful Tales

"Kill me," said the poor creature, and he bowed his head towards the water and awaited his death. But what did he see reflected in the transparent water?

He saw below him his own image, but he was no longer a clumsy dark gray bird, ugly and ungainly. He was himself a swan! It does not matter in the least having been born in a duckyard, if only you come from a swan's egg.

The story of the ugly duckling is one of the best loved of children's stories. It is the story of a poor creature who was plagued with ugliness and ungainliness even before his hatching. The mother duck was puzzled because the egg was large and had not hatched long after the other ducklings were waddling around. When it finally hatched, the duckling was so big and ugly that the mother thought he must be a turkey. He could swim as well as the other ducklings, though, so she tried to encourage him.

The duckling was criticized and attacked by the other ducks until he finally decided to leave. At a nearby lake he met wild ducks, who also considered him quite ugly but agreed to accept him so long as he did not intermarry! Attacked by hunters, the ugly duckling was nearly grabbed by a dog, but miraculously escaped. He leaves the scene thinking that he is too ugly even for a vicious dog.

The duckling came to a cottage where a cat and hen lived with an old woman. They tried to teach him to purr and cluck, but to no avail; and if he cannot purr or cluck, he is of no value at all. He left the cottage to live in a lake, but was nearly

The Ugly Duckling

frozen to death in the ice covered water. A peasant rescued him and took him home. Reviving, the duckling flew around making a shambles of the house. Finally he escaped from the house to return to a miserable existence in the winter.

Early in the spring the duckling saw some beautiful swans and decided to swim over to them, fully expecting to be killed by them for his impudence. As he approached them, he bowed his head for the onslaught he expected from them. In the water he saw his own image. He himself was also a beautiful swan! The others honored him for his youthfulness and beauty. "He was happy, but not at all proud, for a good heart never becomes proud."[1]

"The Ugly Duckling" is, fundamentally, a Cinderella story. It is the account of one who was completely misunderstood by all of those near to him. Finally his genuine beauty and grace are discovered when his own kind recognize him. His misery until that recognition is almost overwhelming. This is the story of the ridicule and persecution of one who did not fit the normal customary expectation. He was too large and, therefore, ugly. He could not purr like a cat or cluck like a chicken and, therefore, was impossibly stupid.

The Ugly Duckling is not arrogant or rebellious as was the Gingerbread Man. He is not inexperienced, as was Chicken Little. In the story of Chicken Little, there is a fundamental misunderstanding because Chicken Little mistook a nut for a piece of the falling sky. Here a baby swan is mistaken for a duckling, though a very ugly one. In Chicken Little tragedy strikes in the form of Foxy Loxy as the "sky is falling" story is told over and over. The tragedy in "The Ugly Duckling" comes from persecuting those whom we do not understand. "How ugly that duckling is! We won't stand him."[2] So a duck attacked him. To which his mother protested, "He is doing no harm." The answer came, "But he is so ungainly and queer that he must be whacked."

The problem is deeper than misunderstanding. It may represent rebellion, but rebellion of a special kind. There is a perverse absence of compassion. What we do not understand, or what does not fit our normal categories, we attack.

This lack of compassion is what Jesus spoke about in the story of the Good Samaritan. Of all Palestinians in the first century, the Samaritans were considered by Israel to be most ugly. The story shows how ugliness is overcome by compassion. Hans Christian Andersen seems to be saying that there is a very pernicious meanness of spirit deep in the human soul.

Christianity has traditionally identified the fundamental human perversity in several different ways. One view is that humanity is ignorant, not wise enough to know the will of God. Chicken Little exemplifies human ignorance. A second view is that the human problem is located in the will rather than the intellect. Humanity is unwilling to service God. Human kind has rebelled against God and is incapable of doing otherwise. Every human project is tainted with the bondage of self-destruction. The Gingerbread Man is a good example. Karl Barth has suggested that the predominant modern sinfulness is lack of feeling and compassion for our brothers and sisters. Apathy is the modern sin.

Apathy or lack of compassion does include ignorance, for there is a misperception of the other person. It also includes rebellion, for there is a perverse intention against the other. At root it is a denial of the feelings we have as fellow human beings. The Ugly Duckling is a good example of apathy and lack of compassion for a fellow creature.

There are obvious parallels between the life of Hans Christian Andersen and the story of the Ugly Duckling. Whether the story is intentionally autobiographical is not certain. There is no way of being sure. There are parallels, however, between the story and Andersen's life.

Hans Christian Andersen was born in Odense, Denmark, April 2, 1805, the son of a poor cobbler. While a boy he was considered a fool and a dreamer. Tall for his age, he was awkward and homely, and often the butt of jokes and pranks from his companions. The relationship to the Ugly Duckling in the duckyard, ridiculed by his playmates is obvious. Young Hans would often listen to his father read aloud to him, an activity that apparently gave him his love for storytelling and the theater.

Andersen left home at the age of fourteen to seek a career in Copenhagen. His attempt to work his way into theater life was met largely with laughter and ridicule. This parallels the ridicule of the Ugly Duckling by the wild ducks at a nearby pond.

By good fortune Hans at seventeen came to the attention of a director of the Royal Theater, who sponsored his further schooling in Slagelse. There he suffered miserably under the taunts of the teacher which produced recurrent nightmares and fear that he was losing his sanity. Again one sees a parallel to the hen, the cat, and the old woman. They could only treat the duckling according to their own expectations until the duckling fled in despair. Andersen's sponsor finally interceded and took him from the school.

Andersen began to publish in 1829. Four years later he received money from the king of Denmark for travel through Europe. In 1835 he published *Fairy Tales For Children,* but he still sought fame as a dramatist. He wrote "The Little Mermaid" and "The Emperor's New Clothes" in 1837 with overwhelming reception. It was only then that he realized that the writing of fairy tales for children was his special talent. Again there is a parallel to the duckling's suffering in the lake, freezing, and being saved by a sponsor. In the spring the duckling sights the swans and goes to them expecting to die. Instead they honor him. Andersen began to recognize that in his fairy tales he was to receive great honor.

The parallels between the story of the Ugly Duckling and Andersen's life may be strained. However the feelings of the duckling that he was awkward and unwanted and that he must suffer until recognized, are more than accidentally related to Andersen's experience. Andersen remembered well the suffering of his own childhood and youth, and he was able to express this suffering in his tales.

Some critics suggest that Andersen's tales are not good for children.[3] They are too full of pain and despair, and the main character can do nothing to relieve the tension. The resolution neither comes in death ("The Steadfast Tin Soldier") or in a miraculous recognition ("The Ugly Duckling").

The main character can do nothing to affect the result except to remain steadfast. The result, according to the critics, is a deep underlying mood of despair. They go on to write that Andersen's stories actually feed that despair rather than resolve it.

This is a powerful argument. In fact some children may be depressed by reading Andersen's tales. However most children seem to find hope in the story of the Ugly Duckling because the story points to the way in which we all depend upon the grace of providence in all the choices we make. In Andersen's stories there is a strong suggestion that no matter how difficult the circumstances, God's providence will care for those who do not lose faith.

Undergirding every choice we make is a pre-ethical choice, a willingness to believe in God's grace in the midst of persecution, and a hope that, sometime, the poor in spirit will rejoice. The reason that the story is so widely loved is that every human being knows what it is to be misunderstood and everyone has a sense of inadequacy before the infinite. The gospel story tells us that we are all swans rather than ducks, but we must be willing to bow our heads to the water and die before we recognize that God views each of us in the reflection of Jesus the Christ. It is there we discover that we have been hatched from a swan's egg. The despair comes from trying to recreate ourselves into better ducklings. The discovery that we are God's swans banishes despair.

In a very simple way children hear the story in terms of how it ends. They can tolerate the pain because they anticipate the joy. What Andersen is calling for is not some task, but rather a quality of spirit, a courage that endures suffering. The story gives voice to an experience that children can recognize and, therefore, they love the story.

Consider the story of the Steadfast Tin Soldier. Mishapen from the time he was cast, because there was too little tin, the soldier stood erect upon only one leg. His fancy was caught by a paper ballerina who danced standing upon the toe of one foot. One day the soldier fell from the window to the street below where some children sent him on a perilous ride in a paper boat. Coming to the canal he was swallowed by a fish, which was caught and bought in the market by the cook of the same household where he had originally lived. He was overjoyed to be reunited with his ballerina, but, suddenly, a child picked him up and threw him into the fire. A breeze caught the dancer who also fluttered into the fire. "When the maid took away the ashes next morning she found him in the shape of a small tin heart. All that was left of the dancer was her spangle, and that was burned as black as coal."

The pain in this story is overwhelming, nor is there hope that it will be removed. The hope lies in the tin soldier's returning from perilous boat journey to the side of his beloved ballerina. A certain destiny allows him to know romance, but death cannot be denied. However even there providence allows him to share the presence of the dancer. Hope also is in a certain attitude that is shared by both the soldier and the dancer. Andersen calls it steadfastness. No matter how perilous the experience, the soldier remained steadfast, and in this "he was the very one who became famous."[4]

One seems to catch a hint of Andersen's reference to himself again. Like the mishapen soldier who loved a paper dancer, Andersen was viewed as someone malformed. He cared for three women whom he was not able to marry. But he did remain steadfast and his stories illuminate the experience for others. Unlike the rebellious gingerbread man, the soldier's only fault was that the goblin in the box did not like him. The story gives only a suggestion of hope and is otherwise quite somber.

Another of Andersen's stories is called "The Fir Tree."[5] It tells of a little fir tree in the forest who longed to be grown up, beautiful, and experienced like the big trees. The tree ignored the advice of the sunbeam and the air to rejoice in "the young life that is in thee." When the young tree was cut down and taken into the house as a Christmas tree, it longed to know what would happen next. After Christmas it was thrown into the attic where it told the story of Humpty Dumpty to the mice and longed to be out of the attic. Finally retrieved from the attic it was chopped up and burned as it remembered its youth in the forest, the eve of Christmas, and Humpty Dumpty—at last it was consumed.

The mood of the fir tree is much different from the ugly duckling. The theme seems to be this: rejoice in the life that is in you at any stage, because soon enough all will be consumed. The tree's only story is Humpty Dumpty, which symbolizes that to fail to experience the life in you is to find life irretrievably shattered. This is not the story of an ugly duckling fir tree which was discovered to be beautiful at Christmas eve. Rather, the tree is beautiful from the beginning, except that his discontent hides it from him. His moment of glory on Christmas eve is also clouded by his own discontent rather than being persecuted and misunderstood by others, as was the duckling. Here is one who missed life because he did not allow it to be. He was so caught in the discontent of each passing stage of life that he could not enjoy the glory and wonder of living. Andersen speaks directly to the youth who always want to get on with the next life stage.

Again as in the stories previously mentioned, one senses a melancholy about the enjoyment of life, which seems much like trying to scoop up water with a sieve. Andersen does not avoid the realization that life quickly passes, nor does he hesitate to describe death. Life is like a fire that quickly consumes everything in its path. The critics find it offensive to speak to children of death so forthrightly. But children do know about death. Protecting them from such stories is to protect them from profound living.

There is, however, a note of hope in the story of the fir tree. The tree did have the wonder and glory of life, and it could be in touch with these in memory even as life passed. There is also the hope that the hearer will let life be, will listen to the sun and the air. The message is close to the words of Jesus, "If God so clothes the grass of the field, which today is alive and tomorrow is thrown into the oven, will he not much more clothe you, O men of little faith?"[6]

In the story of the emperor's new clothes Anderson uses a theme of which he was very fond, the foolishness of pride and arrogance. The story is actually an old folktale, but Andersen's retelling is unparalleled in bringing the characters to life.

Simply put, the story is about a king who was taken in by two swindlers. Knowing the king's insatiable desire for new clothes they offer to weave cloth that had "the peculiar quality of becoming invisible to every person who was not fit for the office he held, or who was impossibly dull."[7] The imposters proceeded to weave the imaginary cloth and fit the invisible new clothes on the emperor. No one dared say that she or he saw no cloth at all, for that would brand the person as either unfit or dull. Each person pretended to admire the very fine clothes of the emperor, until a child said, "But he has got nothing on."[8] Immediately everyone, including the king, knew it to be true, but even then no one dared admit it.

The Emperor in his new clothes

Andersen unmasks the sham of arrogance in this way. He has little sympathy for the proud, those who think themselves better than others. The innocent child is the only one who sees through the sham, and speaks the truth. The virtues of truth, love, steadfastness, humility, courage, and joy run through his stories. One does not come to these qualities by grasping life or by overcoming a hurdle. Nor can the passing of life and the inevitability of death be stayed, for all life is consumed. The stories cannot eliminate pain, but they can introduce the hearer to a new way of experiencing life. They can show the qualities of the soul for which there is no rule, but only the vitality of the spirit.

Should children then not hear the story of the Little Match Girl who freezes to death while trying to gain a few pennies selling matches for her father? Should children not hear about the burning of the Fir Tree or the melting of the Steadfast Tin Soldier? Children will be the poorer if they do not hear these stories. So many children in the world are abused, bullied, injured, and threatened by destruction that Andersen's stories can give a confidence to them. In hearing them a child is in the presence of a gentle storyteller who knows both the pain of life and the simple joy of childhood. Neither are glossed over in the stories. It is for that reason so many children have loved them and found hope in them.

Some children may not like such painful stories, and of course such children should be spared the telling. For that matter a diet of only Andersen's tales might be thin for most children. But sprinkled in with other stories Andersen's add an irreplaceable saltiness. They reach for the source of life that is not controlled by the diligence of our efforts, but which can sustain us in both joy and sorrow. Without often speaking about God, Hans Christian Andersen knows very well how to point in the right direction.

Notes

1. Hans Christian Andersen, *Fairy Tales,* (New York, NY: Grosset and Dunlap, 1965), p. 82.

2. Andersen, *Fairy Tales,* p. 73.
3. For example, Bettelheim, *Enchantment,* pp. 104-105.
4. Andersen, *Fairy Tales,* p. 269.
5. Hans Christian Andersen, *The Complete Hans Christian Andersen Fairy Tales,* edited by Lily Owens (New York: Avenel Books, 1981), pp. 1-6.
6. Matt. 6:30 *RSV.*
7. Andersen, *Fairy Tales,* p. 263.
8. Andersen, *Fairy Tales,* p. 68.

·5·

The Edge of Forever

The rain is raining all around,
It falls on field and tree,
It rains on the umbrellas here,
and on the ships at sea.[1]

Part of Robert Louis Stevenson's appeal is to be able to take the very common experiences of childhood and to transform them into something of beauty and wonder. He writes of swings, bedtime, windy nights, rain, train rides, shadows, the seasons, and many other very common experiences. Yet when Stevenson writes about them, the memories of childhood come flooding back to us. Thoughts we had long since forgotten become vivid. Stevenson was able to catch the child's excitement in these experiences. He also caught the fear and the wonder, the imagination and the delight. His few lines about the rain beautifully reflect the mood of a rainy day.

Robert Louis Stevenson is sometimes given credit for being the first to write poetry for children instead of about them. His *A Child's Garden of Verses* is a classic collection of poems written from the point of view of a young child. Their appeal is so universal that children and adults alike enjoy hearing them again and again. I have selected several examples of Stevenson's poetry for children and look into the meaning and mood they convey. In the next chapter I will contrast these poems of Stevenson with some of the poems and stories of A. A. Milne, who is also an enormously popular writer for children. We can consider together, then, the vision of the gospel in dialogue with the vision of these two poet storytellers.

Stevenson wrote with marvelous imagery. Consider the poem, "From a Railway Carriage":

Faster than fairies, faster than witches,
Bridges and houses, hedges and ditches,
And charging along like troops in a battle,
All through the meadows the horses and cattle:
All the sights of the hill and the plain
Fly as thick as driving rain;
And ever again, in the wink of an eye,
Painted stations whistle by.[2]

The contrasting images in the poem come as quickly as the train ride itself. Many of the images are similes rather than actual descriptions: fairies, witches, troops in a battle, driving rain, wink of an eye, "painted" stations. The similes almost overwhelm the designations: bridges, houses, hedges, ditches, meadows, horses, cattle, hill, and plain. The mixture of similes and designations contribute to both the variety and the mood of the ride.

The meter is equally seductive. "Faster than fairies" sets the timing of a heavy stroke followed by two light strokes. That particular meter gives a strong sense of racing along. It matches the clickety-clack of the train wheels on the track. The racing meter and the collage of images combine to picture the mood of a real train ride.

Stevenson's style is characterized by a strong contrast of concrete and imaginative images. We have just considered the interplay of similes and designations. One can also think of them as concrete and imaginative. In the poem "The Rain," quoted above, he refers to rain, fields, trees and umbrellas, all of which are commonly experienced images. Then he mentions the ships at sea, which enormously expands the domain of the rain. The particular is enlarged by the imaginative.

The same interplay is seen in the poem "The Land of Counterpane."

I was the giant great and still
That sits upon the pillow-hill,
And sees before him, dale and plain,
The pleasant land of counterpane.[3]

A sick child is in bed imagining that the bedclothes are a series of hills and valleys. On the bedclothes the child plants soldiers and ships, houses and cities. He views the make-believe land in the bedclothes from the point of view of a "giant great and still." I recently discovered that a counterpane is a bed cover or comforter. The interplay of imagination and experience is picked up in phrases like "pillow-hill," and "dale and hill (in the) land of counterpane."

The psychological appeal of the "garden of verses" is to experiences such as delight, play, safety, fear of the dark, and a sense of wonder. Throughout all experiences the child is constantly exercising imagination. From a more modern perspective the child is trying to establish a sense of dependable self-identity over against the many impulses, delights, and fears of everyday experience.

A sense of self-identity is especially evident in the poem "A Good Boy."

I woke before the morning, I was happy all the day,
I never said an ugly word, but smiled and stuck to play.

Not saying ugly words and sticking to play, to say nothing of smiling, are things the child is expected to do and is trying to do. At the end of the day the child is happy because "I know I have been good."

I know that, till tomorrow I shall see the sun arise,
No ugly dream shall fright my mind, no ugly sight my eyes.[5]

The experience of intruding ugly dreams and ugly sights are something every five or six-year-old child knows. The child is learning to know that there is a dependable world, signaled by the fact that at night one can trust that the sun will rise in the morning. It is reminiscent of Martin Luther's "Now I lay me down to sleep, I pray the Lord my soul to keep." There, also, the sense of dependability overcomes the sense of fear in the night at bedtime.

The fear of night time is also expressed in the poem "Northwest Passage."

The shadow of the balusters, the shadow of the lamp,
The shadow of the child that goes to bed—
All the wicked shadows coming, tramp, tramp, tramp,
With the black night overhead.[6]

The morality of these poems reflect a strict Scottish upbringing. Modern parents would hardly insist that their children never say an ugly word, smile, and stick to play. Nor would most parents consider that the whole duty of children is to say what's true, speak when spoken to, and behave mannerly at the table.[7] The child in Stevenson's garden is learning a much stricter code than many children learn in our day. For that reason, some of the poems seem very quaint.

Nevertheless, learning to be dependable in expected ways is a universal task of six and seven-year-old children. A more modern image of the same experience is found in Dr. Seuss's "Cat in the Hat."[8] There the children want to play out the imaginative and impish designs suggested by the Cat in the Hat. However the fish in the bowl keeps telling them that they must not do that. What will their mother say when she returns? Many storytellers may want to give up the strictness of Stevenson's idea for children's responsibilities, but they need not abandon his accurate description of many childhood experiences.

The larger point of view of Stevenson's poems is not from a child's perspective but an older man looking back at childhood. That becomes clear in the epilogue "To Any Reader." You cannot recover the child of these verses because

He has grown up and away,
And it is but a child of air
That lingers in the garden there.[9]

Stevenson dedicates the poems to Alison Cunningham, his nurse. He calls her "my second Mother, my first Wife, the angel of my infant life."[10] Often his nurse is mentioned in the poems.

Born in Edinburgh, Scotland in 1850, Stevenson was a sickly child who spent much of his early years confined to bed. Perhaps that confinement contributed to his imagination. The poems are written in the setting of a financially comfortable family, who can afford a nurse and a gardener. There is no sense of financial need. Stevenson seems not to have been nearly as close to his parents as he was to his nurse. He appears to have enjoyed the comfort of his home,

"The Swing"

same time, he had a constant desire to explore the wider world. As a grown man Stevenson fulfilled this childhood dream to explore, finally spending his latter years in the south seas, where he died and is buried.

The meaning of many of Stevenson's poems turns upon what might be called liminal experiences. Liminal experiences are those in which the here and now are juxtaposed with the infinite. Paul Tillich might call them boundary experiences. Such a juxtaposition is to be found in so many of the poems. In "The Swing" the child goes up in the air and over the wall 'til he can see the whole countryside. Then he is brought down to his own garden again, so the alternation between the small locality around the swing and the vastness of the countryside. Swinging is a liminal experience because it permits one to alternate between what is right here and what is far and wide.

Stevenson's poetry is full of such liminal experiences. Where do the boats go? "On goes the river, and out past the mill, Away down the valley, Away down the hill." And when he climbs the cherry tree in the poem "Foreign Lands," what does he see? "I held the trunk with both my hands and looked abroad on foreign lands." The river leads to the sea. The rain rains on you and me, and on the ships at sea. Bedtime is also a liminal experience. It is the boundary between the here and the beyond, this little space and the land of Nod. The seashore is liminal. The little holes in the sand dug by the child can allow the infinite sea to come up in them. The train is liminal because it allows a whole variety of experiences, each of which is here for a fleeting moment. "Each glimpse and gone forever." Such liminal experiences come in nearly all of the poems; one can hardly exhaust the list of such experiences. It gives a sense of wonder to even the most mundane experience.

The wonder of these poems is the spacially infinite, the temporally transient, and the experientially inexhaustible. The infinite beckons, and for the most part is not fearsome. Extended space leads to strange people in strange places. Time washes out every experience so that in a moment each particular is gone. The mill wheel will "keep roaring and foaming forever long after all the boys are away." When the boys are old, with the beans and marbles of childhood in hands, they shall meet at the ever churning mill wheel and remember the past. Memory brings bittersweet reveries; the sweetness of childhood delight recalled, the bitterness that all is gone forever.

Seldom do we get a personal image of the liminal. Occasionally there are personal suggestions. "The wicked shadows coming tramp, tramp, tramp." Of the wind he writes:

O you that are so strong and cold,
O blower, are you young or old?
Are you beast of field and tree,
Or just a stronger child than me?[11]

One gains a great sense of questioning about the beyond, but certainly not dread. Only in the "Unseen Playmate" do we get a very personal image of the one who is called "the friend of the child." In that rare poem the infinite is very personal.

Stevenson was reared in a Christian home, although his references to being Christian are mostly a matter of praying and behaving conventionally. It is nice to think of "little children saying grace in every Christian kind of place." However, Stevenson's vision parallels the Christian gospel in ways that are much more than conventional. The sense of wonder and trust in a power beyond our finite world is basic to the gospel. The presence of that power in all of the small moments of our lives is also like the gospel.

The fleeting glimpse of the personal in "The friend of the child" is like Jesus addressing God as "Abba, Daddy" in the beginning of the Lord's prayer. The gospel's love of children is to be seen in Jesus' saying, "Except you become as little children, you cannot enter the Kingdom of Heaven." Or again Jesus rebuked the disciples for keeping the children from him, "for of such is the Kingdom of Heaven." Stevenson's image of children as curious, imaginative, observant, trustful, loving, expectant, and sometimes afraid all serve as a commentary on Jesus' saying, "except you become as a little child . . ."

His delight in the commonplace is like the parables of Jesus, who could see the presence of the kingdom in very common experiences. Jesus likened the Kingdom of God to a woman sweeping her house to find a coin, to a farmer planting grain, and again to a wedding ceremony. The lilies of the field, the rain, the birds, and the seasons were signs of God's trustworthiness in the rain, flowers, birds, and seasons.

However, there is also a note of difference. In Stevenson's vision there is a quizzical wonder about the variety of things. The Bible describes space as nourishing humanity to form a community. The rain is not only a sign of the beyond, but of the fairness of God. The flowers are not only a sign of the infinity of beauty, but of God's clothing us. A farmer planting is not only a sign of the transiency of time, but an anticipation of the harvest, and the harvest itself is a sign of God's reign.

Time for Stevenson seems to be a sheer juxtaposition of the finite and the infinite in a given moment. One is greeted with the disappearance of all particulars in time. There is a wonder, a reverie about the passing of all things. A similar juxtaposition of the infinite and the finite is to be found in Søren Kierkegaard; however, for Kierkegaard the moment is a matter of fear and trembling. In the gospel time reveals a direction, a purpose, a promise of consummation. The garden of verses contains a curiosity about the beyond, indeed a romantic drive to experience the beyond, but there is neither dread nor the hope of fulfillment in a community of love.

The expectation of the reign of love and justice is not there. Perhaps I am asking too much to even suggest that it might be there in poetry for children. And yet in a deeper sense the writing of the poetry itself is an anticipation of the community of love. Stevenson hoped that his poetry would be read to children, and that they "may hear it in as kind a voice as made my childish days rejoice." Like the gospel, the retelling of the story is an act of love between teller and hearers, and it too is a passing moment that stands in the wonder of the infinite. In fact, the gospel anticipation of a wider community of love that appears absent from the poems is embodied in the act of writing and telling.

In order that such observations do not seem presumptuous, let me hasten to add that the poems themselves have their own beauty and delight that far outweighs any observations made about them. We cannot judge the heart of the poet, but we can look at ways in which the poetic images are parallel to the gospel images.

Notes

1. Robert Louis Stevenson, *A Child's Garden of Verses*, (New York: The Platt and Munk Co., 1932), p. 25.
2. Stevenson, *Garden*, p. 18.
3. Stevenson, *Garden*, p. 19.
4. Stevenson, *Garden*, p. 14.
5. Stevenson, *Garden*, p. 14.
6. Stevenson, *Garden*, p. 33.
7. Stevenson, *Garden*, p. 29.
8. Dr. Seuss, *The Cat in the Hat*, (New York: Random House, Inc. 1957).
9. Stevenson, *Garden*, p. 84.
10. Stevenson, *Garden*, p. 5.
11. Stevenson, *Garden*, p. 29.

·6·

A Community of Character

It's ever so portant how you walk.
And it's ever so jolly to call out, "Bears,
Just watch me walking in all the squares."[1]

The work of A. A. Milne stands in striking contrast to that of Robert Louis Stevenson. Milne also wrote for children, and his writings also seem destined to be considered classics. Many, many children have and continue to get great delight from the Winnie the Pooh poetry and stories. However the experience for the listening child is likely quite different from hearing *A Child's Garden of Verses.*

The Winnie the Pooh stories consist of a father telling stories to his son who with his toys are becoming the principal characters of the story. The stories are written to delight a child rather than for an adult to recall the happy experiences of childhood. All the experiences are therefore imaginary rather than the interweaving of fantasy and actual event. Milne's Christopher Robin seems to be about the same age as Stevenson's child in the garden, perhaps six, seven, or eight. But Christopher Robin's adventures occur in an imaginary forest rather than actual beds, houses, and lawns.

In a typical story Winnie the Pooh sets out to find honey for his insatiable bearish appetite.[2] Happening upon the burrow of his friend Rabbit, Pooh invites himself in over Rabbit's objections. Furthermore, Pooh manages first to get Rabbit to serve him some honey and then, finally, consumes all of Rabbit's store of honey. Pooh is then so stuffed from eating that he cannot get out of Rabbit's door. They call upon Christopher Robin who suggests that nothing can be done except to wait for Pooh to get thin again. By the end of a week Pooh is thin enough that Christopher Robin, Rabbit, and all of Rabbit's friends were able to pull him out of the door.

This story, like the other Pooh stories, is about such everyday occurrences as visiting a friend, eating too much, getting stuck, and having to be helped out. A child can easily identify with all of this. With the exception of Christopher Robin, the characters are talking animals which also delight most children. However, beyond the storyline and the setting, the delight is in the dialogue.

The dialogue is full of rhymes and nonsense syllables and sounds, as is often found in the Mother Goose rhymes. For example, as Pooh walked along he sang:

Tra-la-la, tra-la-la,
Rum-tum-tiddle-um-tum.

There is also a constant use of word play and logical puzzles that is reminiscent of *Alice in Wonderland.* This can be illustrated with the first interchange between Rabbit and Pooh. Please remember that Rabbit is not at all eager for Pooh to come in because Rabbit is fully aware of Pooh's enormous appetite. Bending down into Rabbit's entrance, Pooh asks,

> "Is anyone at home?"
>
> There was a sudden scuffling noise from inside the hole, and then silence.
>
> "What I said was, 'Is anybody at home?' " called out Pooh very loudly.
>
> "No!" said a voice; and then added, "You needn't shout so loud, I heard you quite well the first time."
>
> "Bother," said Pooh. "Isn't there anyone there at all?"
>
> "Nobody."[3]

Milne is able to derive great humor out of the situation in which Pooh wants in and Rabbit tries to keep him out. Part of the humor is the paradox of someone saying that no one is there. Part of the humor is in the great courtesy with which they cover their basic interests. Part of the delight is the naturalness of the emotions and the vividness with which they are described. Children can identify with the situation, but many adults also appreciate the curious paradoxes and turns of language.

The basic motives of the stories are very elemental: hunger, curiosity, protecting one's own, companionship, helplessness, confusion, willingness to help. These are motives with which most children can identify. There is, as well, an underlying note of conflicting impulses. Pooh struggles with himself to remain civil, as does Rabbit. Then there is the rather direct, albeit courteous, conflict between Pooh and Rabbit. The animals are trying to get some distance from their own immediate emotions, something very characteristic of four-, five-, and six-year-old children. Basically they are not successful, whereas Christopher Robin is. He is more mature, having established the ability to be more nearly in control of his deeper impulses. The very presence of Christopher Robin helps the animals resolve their basic conflicting emotions.

One could ask whether Christopher Robin is not wasting too much time in reverie in the imaginary forest rather than tending to his homework. Is there not a certain arrogance in the way that Christopher Robin is able to come into situations and quickly resolve them with a condescending, "Silly Old Bear," and a pat on the head? I can't really accept this argument. The fact is that all children do go through such a phase, and the stories carry the hope that more maturity will resolve such issues.

The social setting of the stories is the conflict of various temperaments. Bear, Rabbit, Eeyore, Owl, and the others all have rather well defined character roles and dispositions that are constantly at odds with one another. The stories question whether people can adjust to one another's intransigent peculiarities while at the same time genuinely caring for one another. The animals need one another as much as they annoy one another.

Children at the age of Christopher Robin are learning what it is to be fair. In fact they can be very legalistic about what is and is not equal for all. Since the Pooh stories are about conflict of interest, the question of fairness is always somewhere in the background. Milne works at the question more in terms of the consequences of behavior rather than strict rules. There is a pervading sense that bad mistakes and even unfavorable consequences can be endured. When Pooh wants to know whether he is stupid, Christopher Robin assures him that, indeed, he is not stupid, only a rather silly old bear. Selfishness will get one into trouble, but all is not lost.

Milne's stories contain many gospel-like characteristics, but they are considerably different from those of Robert Louis Stevenson. The gospel is the story of God's formation of a human community in the face of a great deal of human intransigence. In his stories Milne has a community dimension that is nearly missing in Stevenson's *A Child's Garden of Verses.* If Stevenson has an underlying trust in the infinite then Milne expresses an underlying hope that all conflict finally will be resolved. In the gospel the trust in the One beyond us is also the hope that our community conflicts ultimately will be resolved.

However, the Pooh stories resolve things too nicely and easily. A mere word from Christopher Robin makes everything all right again. There is no sense of the suffering that comes from human conflict. It is an idyllic vision of the shift to maturity which comes with civility, good humor, and intellectual word games. There is also humor and word play in the gospel, but there is also an undercurrent of serious tragic conflict. Jesus' critics are not as easily converted by a few words.

While the Pooh stories deal with consequences, maturing, and the building of human community, they are not as much in touch with the pain of life. Children, too, experience emotional pain. The story of the Gingerbread Man contains an awareness of this kind of pain. The fear of the shadows in Stevenson's garden is more real than the fear of painful consequences in Milne.

The fact is that while Milne is working wholly within an imaginary setting with hope found in very real but playful dilemmas, Stevenson is writing of very real experiences and finding delight in the presence of the invisible. The gospel takes us in very real, physical circumstances, to bring us hope of a community of love in the person of one who experiences our pain and sorrow. I find it interesting that the grown Christopher Robin criticized his father for spending so much time writing stories and so little time actually in touch with him.

In Milne the search for the infinite is usually resolved in a happy, concrete accident. In a story in which Pooh, Piglet, Owl, Eeyore, Rabbit, and Christopher set off to find the North Pole, they are confronted by the fact that no one knows how to identify it.[4] They seem to be searching for the indefinable limit of their forest. The search is resolved when in their search to get across a stream, Pooh finds a pole to assist them. Christopher Robin immediately identifies it as the North Pole. The illusive limit for which they were searching is found in the resolution to a particular community problem.

The themes of character and community are also to be found in Milne's poetry. Take for example this poem, "Lines and Squares" from *When We Were Very Young*.[5] The narrator of the poem is a child who is careful not to walk on the lines, lest the bears devour him. In the preface Milne explains that the narrator is probably Hoo, "one of those curious children who is four on Monday, and eight on Tuesday, and . . . twenty-eight on Saturday."[6]

As long as the child walks on the squares, he is quite safe from the bears. On the other hand, "[T]he little bears growl to each other, 'He's mine, As soon as he's silly and steps on a line.' " Milne is writing of a characteristic that is nearly universal for six- to ten-year-old children. Another rendering is "Step on a crack and break your mother's back."

Freud noted a tendency to compulsiveness in such behavior. He saw it as the child's superego putting restrictions upon unacceptable impulses. However, the point can also be made that both the child and the bears are bound by certain constraints. To learn to depend upon those constraints is basic to all communities. So here again Milne is expressing the child's effort to constrain her or his own behavior in order to relate to another. Even the child's imagination while walking on a London street is a social behavior.

Milne's concern about formation of a caring community, the rebirth of hope in the midst of social conflicts, learning to forgive the foibles of ourselves and others, are also central to the gospel. But the gospel knows the depths of our pain and quickens us to be more sensitive to that ultimate search for meaning in our midst.

Stevenson and Milne approach the gospel story from two different sides. Stevenson can remind us of the trustfulness and unending expanse of God's love while Milne can remind us of the purposefulness and community building character of God's love. Of course, one need not be reminded of the gospel at all in reading the poems and stories. Yet the gospel tells us that both dimensions of God's grace are needed.

"Bears, just watch me walking in all the squares."

Notes

1. A. A. Milne, *When We Were Very Young,* (New York: E. P. Dutton & Co., Inc., 1950), p. 13.
2. A. A. Milne, *Winnie-the-Pooh,* (New York: E. P. Dutton, 1950), pp. 20-31.
3. Milne, *Winnie,* p. 22.
4. Milne, *Winnie,* p. 108-127.
5. Milne, *Very Young,* p. 12-13.
6. Milne, *Very Young,* p. x.

·7·

Delightful Nonsense

"Cheshire Puss," she began... "Would you tell me which way I ought to go from here?" "That depends a good deal on where you want to get to," said the cat. "I don't much care where—" said Alice. "Then it doesn't matter which way you go," said the cat.[1]

Alice in Wonderland is considered to be the first classic written for children in the English language. The story leads Alice through a wonderful array of situations, puzzles, and word plays. The point of all of these seems simply to delight the reader. There seems to be no calculated effort to reform children or give them a moral. Wonderland lives up to its name, a place of remarkable events and great delight.

In spite of its enormous reputation, few children have actually read the book, or, in fact, enjoy it. Those who do like it seem to have been encouraged by some adult, delighted by Lewis Carroll's writing. Many adults have not read the book either but remember images or quotations from the story that they have received from other sources. Such impressions are so unforgettable that *Alice in Wonderland* is not likely to be displaced on the list of children's classics in the Western world.

The story of Alice and her adventures, in the words of the author, "are made up almost wholly of bits and scraps, single ideas which came of themselves."[2] In other words, the story is a scrapbook of sayings, puzzles, and quaint situations that occurred to Carroll at various times. The story, therefore, wanders rather than having a strong plot and resolution.

True, Alice does want to return home, but the plot is almost incidental to the word play. That the reader should fasten upon particular sayings is not coincidental; it is a function of the way the story is pieced together.

The logic puzzles and unusual situations of Wonderland are far more interesting to educated adults than to children. The puzzles are beyond the comprehension of younger children. Youth must find delight in that sort of thing in order to want to read it. Carroll does seem to understand that children are intrigued by rudeness, mild violence, impertinence, and eating. All of these are present in *Alice in Wonderland* in great abundance which can delight both children and adults, if they like this sort of thing.

Charles Lutwidge Dodgson was an unlikely writer of children's stories. For forty-seven years his career was as a don, cleric, and lecturer in mathematics at Christ Church, Oxford University. He was a pedantic lecturer, and his scholarly works in mathematics and logic never received great attention.

Dodgson's fascination with little girls led to his writing the story of Alice. He spent much time entertaining the three daughters of his colleague, Dr. Liddell, but his favorite was Alice. She was the first of a series of friendships with little girls, for each friendship was inevitably terminated as the child grew into young womanhood.

On the famous afternoon, July 4, 1862, on which the story of Alice was told, Dodgson, Reverend Robinson Duckworth, and the three Liddell girls, Lorina Charlotte, Alice Pleasance, and Edith[3] rowed up the Thames River from Oxford to the village of Godstow. They had tea there on the bank of the river and returned home by evening. Apparently they often had made the excursion, and Dodgson entertained the girls by telling stories. What seems to have distinguished this particular afternoon is that Alice asked that the story be written down. She was so persuasive that on that same evening he apparently essayed a first draft of what had been told casually in the afternoon.[4]

The circumstances of the afternoon boating trip make the introductory poem understandable.

For both our oars, with little skill,
By little arms are plied

The girls are attempting to row, with mixed success. Very likely there is a word play on "little," which sounds like "Liddell," the last name of the children.

Ah, cruel Three! In such an hour,
Beneath such dreamy weather,
To beg a tale of breath too weak
To stir the tiniest feather!
Yet what can one poor voice avail
Against three tongues together?

At the urging of the three girls, of whom he was so fond, Dodgeson began to tell a story, though he would have preferred to relax in the dreamy circumstances of the trip. But the girls were insistent, and he could do nothing but acquiesce. When he attempted to tease them and put off the story until next time, they would quickly respond, "It is next time."[5]

The characters of Wonderland evolve in the telling: the White Rabbit, the March Hare, the Queen, the Duchess. That they were related to actual events on the outing ("dull reality") becomes clear in the last several paragraphs of the story. The White Rabbit characterizes the wind rustling the grass. The frightened mouse in the pool is occasioned by the waving reeds in the water beside them. The "tinkling sheep bells" inspired the rattling cups of the Mad Hatter's tea party. The pig-baby's sneeze and the Gryphon's cry evolved from "the confused clamor of the busy farmyard."[6] The Mock Turtle was inspired by the lowing cattle in the meadow. Carroll himself defines the circumstances that inspired the characters of the story with such suggestions.

The introduction and conclusion to *Alice in Wonderland* also suggest that Carroll had a romantic vision of the innocence and delight of childhood which has long since passed away. The memories and dreams of childhood are like "Pilgrim's withered wreath of flowers plucked in a far-off land."[7] That same mood is picked up in the concluding paragraph, in which Carroll is pensive about how an Alice grown mature would keep "the simple and loving heart of her childhood." Perhaps she would tell other children the stories of Wonderland and "feel with all their simple sorrows, and find a pleasure in all their simple joys." In retelling the stories she might recall the simpler joys of her own childhood. These lines carry more than a little suggestion about the pain of adult life.

Dodgson's life had its own pain. Painfully shy in the presence of almost all other adults, his shyness was compounded by a stutter in some circumstances. He was able to relax and become his imaginative, jesting self only in the presence of those little girls who were his friends. Apparently little boys were of no interest to him, for he found them to be raucous and greedy. Perhaps this attitude was the inspiration for the Duchess's baby turning into a pig. One might make too much of these attitudes of the author, and yet Wonderland is a very intimidating place. Few persons could exist in Wonderland with its constant threats of execution without experiencing dismay and, likely, much timidity. The pain and questioning of adult life is more than a little present in Wonderland, but so is the simplicity and naiveté of childhood in the form of Alice.

The story begins with Alice and her sister reading on the bank when a white rabbit runs by. Alice is bored by the reading, and "burning with curiosity," she follows the rabbit across the field and into a rabbit hole, where she finds herself falling. She ends up plopping into Wonderland where her size keeps changing; people are in a hurry without knowing where they are going; everyone is impossibly rude to one another; the conversation is more often nonsense than not; people can be threatened with execution for no reason; and there is no evident way of getting home again. In its own way Wonderland pokes fun at the absurdity of life.

The delightful conversation with the Caterpillar deals with being who one is. To the Caterpillar's question, "Who are you?" Alice can only answer that she is not sure, since she keeps changing. The Caterpillar demands, "Explain yourself," to which Alice replies that she cannot explain herself since she is not herself. Alice insists that changing feels queer to her, and the Caterpillar asks again, "Who are you?" The conversation has come full round without going anywhere.

In this dialogue Carroll moves back and forth between change and identity. Change always seems to trade places with identity, but unless there is identity, there can be no sense of change. Identity and change depend upon one another, for neither can be established in its own right. Here we have Carroll's masterful way of disguising a logic puzzle in a wonderful conversation. The paradox between identity and change is simply acknowledged and the conversation goes on to something else.

The Caterpillar is very peremptory in his questions, whereas Alice is shy. "Who are you?", "Explain yourself!", "It isn't," simply require an answer which the Caterpillar flatly rejects. Alice began to feel "a little irritated at the Caterpillar's making such *very* short remarks."[8] However the Caterpillar's attitude is similar to other characters in Wonderland, many of whom are demanding, and the remainder of whom are quite dominated. We also see that although curiosity and having nothing better to do are Alice's main motivations she can become angry if pushed too far. She can also become as demanding as those around her, but she quickly controls her anger and tries again to find some sense in things while remaining a model of courtesy.

The conversation with the Caterpillar also contains the parody on Robert Southey's poem, "The Old Man's Comforts and How He Gained Them." The original begins in this way:

> You are old, father William," the young man cried,
> The few locks which are left you are grey;
> You are hale, father William, a hearty old man;
> Now tell me the reason, I pray."

Alice's recitation changes the poem to:

> "You are old, father William, the young man said,
> And your hair has become very white;

And yet you incessantly stand on your head—
Do you think at your age, it is right?"

Alice's account leads her and the Caterpillar to disagree whether her vision is "not quite right," or "wrong from beginning to end."

The poem shows Lewis Carroll's ability to take the familiar and alter it to show the absurd. Southey's original work was a meditation upon the verse, "Remember also your Creator in the days of your youth,"[9] (Ecclesiastes 12:1). In Carroll's parody Father William discovers early on that he has no brain, life is full of disagreements, and the strong dominate the weak. Father William, therefore, tires of meaningful questions and threatens the youth, "Be off, or I'll kick you down stairs!"

After the discussion with the Caterpillar Alice goes to the kitchen of the Duchess, where she finds the Duchess nursing a baby, the cook stirring soup, and a grinning Cheshire cat. Alice attempts to make conversation with her best manners. "I didn't know that Cheshire cats always grinned." To which the Duchess replies, "You don't know much." We immediately see that the Duchess has the same temperament as the Caterpillar, who was sharp of tongue and quick to contradict.

The conversation is interrupted as the cook begins to throw everything within reach at the Duchess and the baby. Alice protested politely, "jumping up and down in an agony of terror." The Duchess commands, "... chop off her head!" Alice had mentioned the earth's *axis*, reminding the Duchess of *axes*, which prompted her command. No one notices and the conversation continues. This scene again shows the interweaving of word play, paradoxes of meaning, and Alice's courtesy, within a very violent setting. The threats are real enough, but the violence of the occasion is never realized and, therefore, harmless. By the end of the scene, Alice is twisting the baby as she holds tightly to its right ear and left foot. Again Alice is shown in her innocence to be a part of the mild violence as well. She is not unhappy to learn that the baby is a pig. The author even has Alice suggest that many children might do better as pigs.

Alice and the Cheshire Cat

When Alice is startled seeing the Cheshire cat in a tree, the conversation quoted at the head of the chapter takes place. Alice asks directions and the cat replies that it depends upon where she wants to go. The paradox between-purpose and means is cleverly and sharply posed. In Wonderland no one seems to know where they want to go, although many are rushing to get there. In the words of the cat, "We're all mad here." When Alice protests that she isn't mad, the cat replies, "You must be, or you wouldn't have come here." The cat, although not as belligerent as the Duchess, is hardly courteous. The Cheshire cat gradually vanishes until nothing but the grin is left, perhaps an allusion to pure logic.[10]

Next Alice goes to the house of the March Hare, where he, the Mad Hatter, and a Dormouse are having a tea party. The Hare and the Hatter are as impolite as the other characters. "Your hair wants cutting," said the Hatter. Alice replied, "You should learn not to make personal remarks.

The Mad Hatter's Tea Party

It's very rude." Of course they continue to be unmannerly, and Alice attempts to find a sensible starting point for a conversation. When the Hatter asks, "Why is a raven like a writing desk?" Alice thinks that the riddle is solvable, but it becomes evident that the Hatter has no answer.

When one searches for meaning in Alice's *Adventures in Wonderland,* it is like trying to solve the Mad Hatter's riddle. One suspects that Carroll never intended a meaning. Yet for all its piecemeal character, the episodes show a pattern with the logic and word play in a central place. As Alice said in the beginning, "What is the use of a book without pictures and conversation?"[11]

The logic demonstrates certain fundamental contradictions in life, such as those between identity and change, means and ends, thought and action, meaning and logic. Conversation can be logically precise, and yet meaningless. "... (It) seemed to her to have no sort of meaning in it, and yet it was certainly English."[12] The story contains so many logical inconsistencies, but it seems to say that logic cannot solve the problem of meaning for life. The very aimlessness of the story emphasizes the human need for purpose. Alice gets on best when she simply expresses her feeling. She finally leaves Wonderland when she is disgusted with the King and Queen's trial, and she says so. The characters all attack her, but they are merely playing cards. She is a living person who senses that she is tired of their antics. Logic, then, takes its place within the deeper human purpose, which, the story tells us, should not be reversed.

Underlying the logic is the constant threat of chaos. The strong dominate the weak who can be as greedy and insolent as the strong, if given the opportunity. Yet the injury never seems severe. Carroll's talent was in putting "awful truths in ways that do not crush."[13] Carroll shared the nineteenth century perception that beneath all civility was an unconscious caldron of emotion (Freud), a war of all against all (Hobbes).

Innocence, civility, and courtesy come off quite well. Alice is a delightful child attempting to find significance in chaos and illogic. Whether she matures or not, she remains a model of courtesy in the midst of rudeness. She becomes able to assert herself in the face of shame.

Notes

1. Lewis Carrol, *The Annotated Alice, Introduction and notes by Martin Gardner,* (New York: New American Library, 1960) p. 88.
2. Quoted in Roger Sale, *Fairy Tales and After,* (Cambridge, MA: Harvard University Press, 1978), p. 102.
3. Carroll, *Annotated Alice,* p. 21.
4. Carroll, *Annotated Alice,* p. 22.
5. Carroll, *Annotated Alice,* p. 23.
6. Carroll, *Annotated Alice,* p. 163.
7. Carroll, *Annotated Alice,* p. 23.
8. Carroll, *Annotated Alice,* p. 68.
9. Ecclesiastes 12:1.
10. Carroll, *Annotated Alice,* p. 91.
11. Carroll, *Annotated Alice,* p. 25.
12. Carroll, *Annotated Alice,* p. 97.
13. Sale, *Fairy Tales and After,* p. 124.

·8·

Strange Worlds

"I think you are a very bad man," said Dorothy.

"Oh, no, my dear; I'm really a very good man; but I'm a very bad Wizard, I must admit."[1]

The Wizard of Oz has been enormously popular with American children. The story of Dorothy and the Wizard was written by L. Frank Baum, a jack-of-all-trades who, at times, had been employed as a newspaper reporter. Baum became fascinated with children's stories, writing a prose Mother Goose in 1897 and two years later a book entitled, *Father Goose, His Story*. However it was *The Wizard of Oz* published in 1902 that made Baum famous. The book was so well received that Baum's publisher insisted upon more stories, fourteen in all. Eight of them have been dramatized on stage.

Just as Sir Arthur Conan Doyle tired of writing about Sherlock Holmes, so Baum tired of writing the Oz stories. Critics generally consider that the later stories are not as imaginative as the earlier.[2] In fact, just as Doyle did with Holmes, Baum attempted to write a finish to the Oz books so that no further contact with Oz would be possible. It was a useless ploy. The publisher insisted upon more stories.

Those who have read Baum's book recognize that the movie does not always follow the book, yet the movie scenes are more strongly etched in the memories of most children. The book and the movie are both controversial. Some children find the movie so violent that they are afraid to watch it. In fact in England the movie has been restricted because of its violence.

The controversy over the violence is all the more curious in view of Baum's introduction to the story. He calls for a series of newer wonder tales "in which the stereotyped genie, dwarf and fairy are eliminated, together with all the horrible and blood-curdling incidents devised by their authors to point a fearsome moral to each tale.... (T)he modern child seeks only entertainment in its wonder-tales and gladly dispenses with all disagreeable incidents."[3]

The critics find "disagreeable incidents" aplenty in *The Wizard of Oz*, so much so that many children are severely frightened. Whether there is "only entertainment" is also questionable. In fact, the account that follows suggests that there is a strong sense of the moral in the story. However the moral is not obvious, nor is it as clearly apparent as in a fable. Baum is in the style of Lewis Carroll, who sets out primarily to entertain children. If a moral can be found, it is because the writer cannot help but put something of himself into the story. Oz contains all the wonder of Wonderland, but it lacks the delightful conversations in which Alice was constantly engaged. Dorothy has a clear destination, and Baum is more interested in her journey than her conversations.

Some critics also consider *The Wizard of Oz* to be an attack upon the American dream of achievement through hard work.[4] Presumably this is because the Wizard turns out to be a "humbug" who has deceived the people into building the Emerald City. The Wizard can do none of the things the people think he can. In fact, it is only because they wear their green spectacles that the city looks emerald. Are children being taught that the dreams for which people work are illusion? Quite the contrary is true. The story is full of the optimism of achievement.

The reader should remember that the story begins with Dorothy and her dog Toto living with her family in Kansas. A tornado carries Dorothy and Toto to Oz, where the house lands on the Wicked Witch of the East, killing her. With the help of the Good Witch of the North Dorothy dons the silver slippers and sets off to the Emerald City to find the Wizard so that she and Toto can return to Kansas. She is joined by a scarecrow, a tin man, and a lion along the way. They travel with her, hoping to have their own wishes fulfilled. The scarecrow wants brains, the tin man a heart, and the lion courage.

When, after many difficulties, they reach the Wizard, he requires them to retrieve the golden crown from the Wicked Witch of the West. She, instead, enslaves Dorothy's friends, but cannot harm Dorothy because of the blessing of the Good Witch of the North. Finally, an angry Dorothy throws water on the witch, only to discover that water melts her. Dorothy and her friends return to the Wizard where they are surprised to find that he is a powerless old man. He is a symbol, though, of the fact that they already have the wisdom, feelings, and courage they desire. But he cannot help Dorothy. She and her friends then travel to the Good Witch of the South, who reveals to her that the silver slippers will take her back to Kansas.

In spite of the constant series of awful obstacles Dorothy faces, she is able to achieve what she sets out to do. Her goal is to return home. Each dilemma she faces has a solution. When the Munchkins cannot help her, she goes to the Wizard. Enslaved by the Wicked Witch of the West, Dorothy melts her with a bucket of water. When the Wizard cannot help, she goes to Galenda, the Good Witch of the South. There she discovers that the silver slippers can take her home. Similarly, a solution is found for the problems of the straw man, the tin man, and the lion. Dorothy and her friends are all able to accomplish what they set out to do.

Far from debunking the American dream, the story is full of a kind of optimism that cannot be dispelled. *Alice in Wonderland* is sharply different. In a general way Alice wants to return home, but neither she nor any other character in the book seems to have a consistent purpose. In fact purpose is nearly overcome in the deep ambiguities of life. There is a much more tragic sense in Wonderland, although a delightful tragedy. Whether it is tragic or not tragic "doesn't matter a bit," in the words of Alice.[5] *Alice in Wonderland* contains much more of the Augustinian sense of the tragedy of life, while Dorothy in Oz is certain to solve her problems in the long run. Oz is full of the American dream.

Dorothy, Toto, and friends

Dorothy, however, cannot solve her problems unless destiny helps. She is not simply pulling herself up by her own bootstraps. The impassable desert around Oz makes it impossible for her to leave without help. The Wicked Witch of the West would destroy her except for the protective kiss on her forehead by the Good Witch of the North. Dorothy must learn to cooperate with destiny and continue to believe that everything will work out. Dorothy is trying to solve the problem of returning home. Alice by contrast is trying to make some sense of the whole situation.

The stories reflect the differences between European and American Christianity. European Christianity has had a much greater tragic sense of life. Christ is the one who saves us from the tragedy of our self-destruction. American Christianity has a stronger sense of cooperating with God's providence. In Christ we have the kiss of God's blessing, but we must continue to work out our salvation.

The American character of Oz is evident in many ways. Richard J. Amundson (professor of history at Columbus College, Columbus, Georgia) has suggested that the story is an allegory which refers to the United States political controversy over whether to coin gold or silver. The story was written at the turn of the century when the question of the gold standard was being hotly debated. William Jennings Bryan ran for president as the hero of the gold standard and the populist movement.

Amundson further suggests that the witches of the North, South, East, and West symbolized dominant economic interests in the United States. The East represented the economic control of Wall Street, and the West mining interests in gold. East and West joined forced in an ill-fated coalition to control the country. The North represented industrial interests, and the South agricultural interests. In the eyes of author Baum, then, the unity of agriculture and industry would solve the nation's problems, according to Amundson.

Dorothy's friends, says Amundson, were symbols for the people who were controlled by regional economic interests. The tin man who chopped down the trees demonstrated how persons are mechanized by industrial life. Industrial society lacks compassion. The straw man represented the farmers, who were not wise enough to solve their own problems. In the lion Amundson sees William Jennings Bryan, popular with the people, but lacking courage.

Dorothy and her friends following the yellow brick road to the Emerald City were like the people who went to Washington in hope that the gold standard would solve all their problems. Amundson hypothesizes that the Wizard was meant to be President McKinley, who was supposed to have power to solve the economic problems, but in fact he did not. Each group had its own perception of the power of the president, all of which were wrong.

Dorothy was sent to the West to bring back the golden crown, in other words to take away the economic power of the West. She was able to do this, but the president cannot solve her problem. The South allowed the silver interests (silver slippers) to overcome the gold interests. This brought Dorothy back to Kansas, but she lost the silver slippers in the process. The implication is that the silver standard could not solve, finally, the economic problems. The real hope lay in the compassion (heart) and wisdom (brain) of industry and agriculture together.

The parallels between the story and the American political scene at the turn of the century are striking. Whether these parallels are really behind the story, or whether Baum actually intended them is very difficult to say. An allegory can be taken in so many different directions that all things become possible. However Amundson's interpretation is very persuasive.

Dorothy's friends may also be considered to be the three parts of the human soul. Classically, the soul has three parts: wisdom, courage and emotion. In Plato's *Republic* a society is just and a person is whole only when the three parts of the soul are evenly balanced. The straw man's desire for wisdom, the lion's lack of courage, and the tin man's need for emotion represent the three classical needs of humanity. Dorothy and her friends can be whole only when they have all three.

An earlier chapter described how Christianity has moved between these three possibilities in locating the basic human problem. Some interpreters of the Roman Catholic tradition have insisted that human sin is a matter of ignorance. The Augustianian and Protestant traditions have held, rather, that the problem of sin is a matter of will. This is traditionally described as rebellion, and therefore, evil is rebellion against God's will. Some writers (e.g., Paul Tillich) suggested that the evil will is a lack of courage (*The Courage to Be*). More recently, writers (Karl Barth) have described human evil as a lack of commpassion or emotion. The friends of Dorothy represent the basic faults of humanity.

The story depends much upon discovering the illusionary character of both hopes and fears. The Wizard is a symbol of hope that the most basic human desire can be satisfied, yet he does not finally have that power. He is a bumbling, balding, old man who can do very little else than direct Dorothy and her friends to face their greatest fears, i.e., to go to the

Dorothy and her friends with the Wizard of Oz

Wicked Witch of the West. All of the hope, wonder, and mystery of the Wizard are illusionary. Furthermore, the great mystery of the Emerald City turns out to be only the result of wearing the green-tinted glasses.

The Wizard is not an evil man, nor does he wish anyone harm. If he appears to be a humbug and an opportunist, one must remember that he does get Dorothy and her friends to face their fears, and he does find a way of giving the friends just what they wanted. He finds a symbolic way of giving brains to the straw man, a heart to the tin man, and courage to the lion.

The story indicates that the friends of Dorothy already have what they want although they are unaware of it. The straw man is gaining experience, so necessary to wisdom. Courage is not an absence of fear, but a willingness to act in spite of fear. The lion has that. The tin man has deep feelings for his friends, and only needs the assurance that it is true. Even Dorothy's return to Kansas depends upon her discovering the power in the silver slippers she has worn throughout the story. The real human hope is not in illusion and sorcery, nor is real human frailty in imagined destruction. Hope comes by facing fear and finding the wisdom, courage, and compassion that is already present and available in life. Finally, the power of good is greater than the power of evil.

The theme of the power of blessing already present in life is very much evident in the Bible. Time and again in the biblical stories someone wants a miracle to show that God's blessing is present, and time and again they must learn that the divine blessing is present beyond the miracle. Moses went to the Pharoah with miracles, but it was God's law that allowed the people to survive. Elijah looked for God in the earthquake, wind, and fire, but God was finally present in the still small voice.

Perhaps the most dramatic example of this is Jesus. The disciples and the people were looking for a powerful conquering king to come as the Messiah. They demanded miracles of Jesus, and he refused as often as he complied. Finally they said that they would believe if he shattered his bonds and came down off the cross. The devil tempted Jesus by calling for a series of miracles, which Jesus refused. To throw oneself off the temple or to turn stones into bread would impress many people, but would not bring them close to the Kingdom of God. When Jesus healed persons, he often said, "Your faith has made you whole." "The Kingdom of Heaven is already among you for those who have eyes to see and ears to hear." People were looking for a great Wizard, and God sent a humble man who pointed to the healing powers already present among them. Frank Baum's *Wizard of Oz* is very close to the gospel narrative in this theme.

Baum also approaches the perspective of the gospel in the facing of one's fear. Dorothy and her friends must go to the one they fear the most, the one who is most likely to destroy them, the Wicked Witch of the West. When they seem hopelessly enslaved, Dorothy has the courage to stand against the witch's power. Just as Gretel realized she must use her intelligence to escape the witch, so Dorothy takes courage in the face of domination, and the domination melts. Dorothy is afraid because she does not understand the power of the blessing she has. Dorothy and her friends remind us of the gospel teaching that the power we have in God's grace and love can overcome all other powers.

Notes

1. Frank Baum, *The Wizard of Oz,* (New York: Rand McNally & Co., 1956), p. 180.
2. Roger Sale, *Fairy Tales and After,* (Cambridge, MA: Harvard University Press, 1978), pp. 226-227.
3. Baum, *Wizard, p. 3.*
4. Sutherland and Arbuthnot, *Children and Books,* 1977, p. 590.
5. Carroll, *Annotated Alice,* p. 156.

·9·

Clever Weakness

" 'Howdy, Brer Rabbit,' sez Brer Fox, sezee. 'You look sorter stuck up dis mawnin,' sezee, en den he rolled on de groun', 'en laughed en laughed twel he couldn't laugh no mo'. "I spek you'll take dinner wid me dis time, Brer Rabbit."[1]

The stories of Joel Chandler Harris (1848-1908) come from the plantation life with which he was familiar as a boy. He loved to listen to stories told by the slaves on the plantation. The beauty of these stories shows not only Harris's love of the stories, but of the storytellers. He recorded the stories in the dialect in which they were told.

The best known of the stories is that of "The Wonderful Tar-baby." Similar stories are to be found in folktales of other people, but none has been so popular as the tar-baby story. It is part of a series of stories that feature Brer Rabbit and Brer Fox. Quick of foot, Brer Rabbit is much weaker than the other animals, so he must use his wits, resourcefulness, and humor to escape being eaten by them.

On this particular occasion Brer Fox decided to outwit Brer Rabbit. By mixing tar and turpentine Brer Fox was able to construct "a contrapshun wat he call a Tar-Baby," which he placed beside the road in wait for Brer Rabbit to come along. Brer Rabbit spoke to the tar-baby. When he received no answer, he slapped it and his paw stuck to the tar face. He struck it again, and again he stuck. Soon he was completely glued to the tar-baby.

At this point Brer Fox appeared and humorously invited Brer Rabbit to dinner. Brer Rabbit, hopelessly trapped, admitted to Brer Fox that he was caught. However, he added that there was one thing he feared more than being eaten by Brer Fox and that was being thrown into the briar patch. Thinking to mete out the worst possible punishment to Brer Rabbit, Brer Fox removed him from the tar-baby and threw him into the briar patch. As Brer Rabbit ran away, safe in his briar patch, he laughed at the way he had tricked Brer Fox into releasing him.

The story is classic in its directness and simplicity. Brer Rabbit has a certain nonchalant self-confidence belying the fact that he always needed to be cautious of his enemies. The jauntiness of Brer Rabbit must have been delightful to the plantation listeners who, as slaves, knew what it was to have to be cautious in order to survive. Brer Rabbit is not malicious, nor is he really devious. He strikes the tar-baby because it does not show the normal courtesy, like a parent reprimanding a child.

Brer Rabbit's error is in his very determination to get respect from the tar-baby. He is so insistent upon getting a pleasant response from the tar-baby that he is oblivious to the danger of the situation. Just as Hansel and Gretel could be enticed by their unrestrained appetites, so Brer Rabbit could be enticed by his need for respect. Since the need for respect is so deeply ingrained, nearly everyone can appreciate Brer Rabbit's insistence. Brer Fox's assessment was correct that Brer Rabbit could not pass by the tar-baby without trying to taunt it in some way.

Once Brer Rabbit was trapped by his own overconfidence, Brer Fox made fun while preparing to eat him. At this point Brer Rabbit came to his senses, realizing that he could be saved only by using his wits. He, too, knew how to read character. By appealing to Brer Fox to save him from the briar patch, Brer Rabbit counted on Brer Fox to want to humiliate him as much as possible. Just as the witch was blind to Gretel's obvious ploy to get the witch to show her how to get into the oven, so the fox was blind to the obvious

Brer Rabbit, Brer Fox and the Tar-Baby

suggestion to throw the rabbit into the briar patch. Greed and desire for mastery blind people to the obvious. Brer Rabbit's courage, cleverness and discernment of Brer Fox's character got him out of the situation.

The theme of the Uncle Remus stories is the survival of Brer Rabbit in the face of overwhelming odds. Brer Rabbit has plenty of faults of his own, and these faults often get him into difficult circumstances. However Brer Rabbit manages to survive through cleverness, courage, humor, and guile. Humiliated, he is not discouraged; captured, he does not despair.

One can understand how these stories would be told and retold by an enslaved people. Black people suffered enormous misery under slavery. Beaten, imprisoned, torn from family, and often required to do backbreaking work, they surely needed encouragement to maintain any kind of self-respect. They had to learn how to survive under an oppressive system and, most of all, how to communicate this to their children. The Uncle Remus stories do this in a humorous and entertaining way.

People under the thumb of an oppressor can seldom speak of their misery directly. It must be disguised by symbolic language, words that do not show outward rebellion to the oppressor. The stories are indirect enough not to provoke the ire of the slave owners, but they do speak directly to the feelings of an oppressed people. They are similar to the Hebrew Bible stories, which also come out of an experience of oppression. In some ways they are like the books of Daniel and Revelation, in which the truth had to be spoken with hidden images so as not to provoke punishment.

The Hebrew stories make clear to us that the experience of slavery touches something in every human soul. The psychologist, Alfred Adler, observed that everyone has feelings of inferiority which motivate human behavior most strongly. The need to be freed from oppression is deeply human. The Hebrew people were always weaker than their neighbors. When the shepherd boy, David, confronted Goliath, it was a contest between weakness and strength. David survived by means of his ingenuity.

The theme of clever weakness is equally important in the New Testament. People were expecting a super hero to rescue them from the oppressive Roman Empire. When Jesus refused to take over the political reins and to mount a military campaign, the people did not understand. At Peter's confession that Jesus is the Messiah, he went on to say that of course Jesus would march into Jerusalem and begin a new political era. Jesus quickly corrected Peter by saying that the Messiah must suffer many things, be crucified, and then rise. Those who follow Jesus follow a way of humiliation, but one that brings great strength and courage. The Apostle Paul spoke of being oppressed on all sides, but not overcome.

The theme of clever weakness can be found in many children's stories. Children are often oppressed and abused, which is why the stories of Uncle Remus appeal to them. James Thurber's story of the princess who wanted the moon illustrates this same theme of strength in weakness.[2]

One evening the princess decided that she wanted the moon and she refused to eat until it was delivered to her. The king didn't know what to do. The wisest men of the kingdom were called in, but they all advised that the moon was too inaccessible to bring to the princess. Finally,the court fool asked why the king seemed to be in despair. When told the story,the fool questioned whether the king had spoken to the princess about the size and composition of the moon. The king sent the fool to talk to the princess who declared that the moon was about the size of her thumbnail and that it was made of silver. The fool had a necklace made to fit the description that the princess had given. She was so delighted that she began to eat again.

Clearly, the princess is a little girl who makes the perceptual mistakes of most preschool children. It appears to her that she can cover the moon with her thumb; therefore, it must be the size of her thumbnail. The king and the wiseman are very literal in their understanding. They spend their time trying to estimate how far away the moon is and how it might be obtained. Only the fool is wise enough to try to understand what the little girl means by her request. It is the fool who really listens to the girl in a way that is helpful to her. The necklace is not, literally, the moon, but it satisfies the princess.

Since the fool in the story appears not to know anything, it gives him opportunity to ask for explanations. Innocent and without understanding, he is, therefore, one who listens intently to those around him. This gives others the freedom to express their own deeper feelings. The fool's understanding and ability to communicate is superior to those who are considered to be wise. His weakness is a source of strength.

The psychologist Jean Piaget has pointed out that preschool children interpret their experience as they perceive it. They believe that far away objects are smaller, and that distant objects move as the person moves. Everyone has seen a mountain move along with a car or train as it moves. The children's experience is tied to its perceptions. By the

The princess who asks for the moon

age of six or seven a child learns to make allowances for their perceptions and that, in fact, distant objects are the same size as those close at hand. They can process the reality that the mountain does not move with the car or train. The princess in the story, probably younger than six, still perceives things as they appear. The king and the wise men had learned to correct their perceptions.

Piaget also noted that adults can think of symbols in their own terms. Children often must have examples in order to understand symbolic patterns. An eight-year-old can tell what time it is by the clock, but an adult can consider what time means. Just as the child older than six no longer distorts immediate perceptions, the adult can reason beyond the distortion of symbols as experienced. In the story the king and wise men were able only to view the facts about the moon. The fool, on the other hand, could ask what the princess meant. The king and the wise men were, therefore, at the level of six- to ten-year-old children. The fool was thinking as an adult.

Often, stories show that the young, the small, or the foolish in their weakness are stronger than the mature, the large, or the wise. The weak must accept their weakness to become strong, and the foolish must accept their foolishness to become wise. The gingerbread man hid his weakness even from himself and was eaten. Hansel and Gretel realized that in their weakness they had to use their intelligence. Dorothy, in the Wizard of Oz, had to discover strength within herself.

Another example is that of Jack and the Beanstalk. This traditional English story is just one of the Jack stories which tell of a bumbling boy who, after many idiotic mistakes learns to be clever enough to care for himself and others. Jack, in his weakness, is destined to overcome the strong. In his ignorance and innocence, he is the wise fool. Unfortunately, Jack represents a traditional male role in that it is the male who must have courage to overcome his own weakness and stupidity. He usually can do this only with female help.

The rhyme of "Jack and Jill" represents the pattern quite nicely. Bumbling as he is, Jack cannot fetch water without falling. Jill is a follower and mother must care for him by wrapping his head. "Jack and the Beanstalk" follows the same theme. In trying to take care of his mother in the absence of the father, Jack symbolizes the traditional closeness of a boy and his mother. However, they are poor and becoming desperate, and Jack is sent to the village to sell a cow. There he meets a man who offers to trade magic beans for the cow, an offer that he accepts. His mother is distraught at his foolishness for Jack has compounded the desperation of their situation.

The mother throws the beans out and, overnight, they grow into a beanstalk that reaches far into the sky. The beans and the beanstalk are obviously masculine symbols. The mother sees only the boy's foolishness, but does not recognize his approaching maturity. His trip up the beanstalk is his tentative first step into the adult world, the land of the giant. Adults seem like giants to children, so they can quickly see the connection between adults and the giants in fairy stories.

The giant is possessive of his realm and resists the youthful Jack's intrusion. Although these emotions are displayed by characters in the never-never land of the beanstalk, they represent feelings that the older generation has about the younger. The giant, who symbolizes Jack's missing father, threatens to eat Jack, but cannot catch him. The underlying anger of the older generation to the younger is evident in this scene.

Inept and bumbling as Jack is, he is able to escape from the giant because of the giant's size and slowness. As one grows older, one tends to become less mobile, whereas the younger generation gains in ability and agility. Inevitably Jack will escape, because in his weakness Jack has an advantage over the giant's strength. His courage allows him to climb the beanstalk into the land of adulthood.

The giant's wife helps Jack to hide when the giant looks for him. She seems to be a split image of Jack's mother. An image that is hard for a boy to imagine is that of his mother as his father's wife. She is not only a figure in his world of childhood, but she also has a role in the adult world. In a similar manner the man who sold Jack the beans for the cow may be a split image of Jack's father as well as the giant. It is not surprising that the giant's wife helps Jack, for helping is the historic role of a mother. The mother's deeper affection for her son shields him from the father's angry impulses. So in his weakness, and with the help of the giant's wife (Jack's mother), Jack escapes destruction. Gradually Jack's lack of wisdom and ineptitude are disappearing.

Jack steals the golden harp and the goose that lays the golden egg from the giant. These are symbols of adult culture. The harp represents music, and the goose represents agriculture and economic productivity. Although youth need to learn the form that sustains the adult world, adults resist turning this knowledge over to the young. Jack's mother expects him to support her. The giant is not willing to give up culture and economics, they must wrest them from their elders. Jack steals what is inherently his.

Jack, chased down the beanstalk by the giant, now has the courage to chop it down. With the death of the giant the division between Jack's world of childhood and adulthood has disappeared. Jack, in entering the adult world, has proved himself a match for the giant while, at the same time, taking over the productive symbols of culture. Jack has accepted his masculinity and his adulthood; consequently, he is now able to care for his mother.

The story of the weak, bumbling Jack who gradually gains the courage and wisdom to confront the strong is an example of clever weakness to be found often in fairy tale stories. A more modern approach to this theme is set in outer space rather than in forests or beanstalks. In earlier chapters it was mentioned that the spiritual crises of other generations were set in the depths of the sea, underground, or in the forest. The current generation is intrigued by outer space, therefore, spiritual crises are now depicted in that setting.

Star Wars is the story of Luke Skywalker who encounters evil in the form of Darth Vadar. In the words of its creator,

George Lucas, "When I developed *Star Wars* I did it as a contemporary fairy tale."[3] Luke is young and apparently weak before the power of Darth Vadar. It is the wise and saintly Ben Kenobie who teaches Luke true strength which does not come so much from physical power as from spiritual discipline. One must learn to trust "the force" that rules the universe. This is not done by becoming stronger and wiser on one's own merits, but by detaching one's self from emotion and pride, and by opening one's self to the experience of the flow of the force. When in *The Empire Strikes Back* Luke is able to sever Darth Vadar's head from the body, the Dark Lord's helmet falls aside to reveal Luke's own face.[4] Luke is not fighting an exterior power, but his own darker side. The powers of darkness are not overcome by great force and strength. They are met in the midst of weakness by surrender to the ruling Force.

The parallel to the gospel is evident and not accidental. Those who follow the way of the cross will submit their wills to the will of God, the power of the Holy Spirit. The world views this as weakness, but to those who know God it is the power of God which, in the end, will overcome the powers of darkness. We are assured of this in that the battle already has been won in the resurrection of Christ. Fairy stories about clever weakness strike a basic theme in human nature, one that is very close to children. Children, in their obvious weakness, are encouraged by these stories. The theme is also deeply centered in the gospel and finds its fullest expression in the weakness of Christ that overcomes the world.

Notes

1. May Hill Arbuthnot, revised by Zena Sutherland, *The Arbuthnot Anthology of Children's Literature,* (Glenview, IL; Scott, Foresman, and Company, 1976), p. 384.
2. James Thurber, *Many Moons,* illustrated by Louis Slobodkin, (New York: Harcourt Brace Janovich, Inc., 1943).
3. Robert Short, *The Gospel From Outer Space,* (New York: Harper & Row, 1983).
4. Short, *The Gospel From Outer Space*, p. 46.

·10·

Reforming the Wolf

"For a long time the silver wolf didn't say anything at all. He just stood there and looked at Barrington with those terrible eyes."[1]

Many of the stories written for children are simply for their delight. Even so, the stories communicate a certain way of looking at things. Frank Baum denies any attempt to moralize, but the *Wizard of Oz* reflects the American penchant for solving practical problems, and it has strong suggestions about how to be in touch with reality. In previous chapters stories are examined for their views of reality, and they are compared to the Christian story. The original writers or editors never may have considered such a comparison.

Another group of stories for children are in the tradition of *Pilgrim's Progress*. They are written intentionally to convey the Christian message. The story may be very imaginative and may use images not found in scripture; nevertheless, the intent is to clarify and illustrate the gospel story. John Bunyan found time to do this when he was cast into prison as a nonconformist. There he wrote about the experiences of the Christian soul. The soul is tempted by "vanity fair," a symbol for the sinful ways of the world. The soul may fall into the "slough of despair," a description of despondency. Bunyan was able to tell this story with all of the drama to be found in the chapbooks of his own childhood, which were the equivalent of today's comics and television. So John Bunyan set the gospel in new images for his time. He did it so well that his story remains a children's classic when the more theological sections are removed.

A modern writer who has attempted to set the gospel into new images is Martin Bell. In *The Way of the Wolf* Bell's wolf represents the enduring power and presence of God. Since the wolf, generally, is given a very bad image in many children's stories, the idea of the wolf as the good and nurturing divine presence is quite different and may be particularly fitting because it still conveys something fearsome and awful. A strong description of God must convey not only God's saving grace, but also the awesome and wonderful power of God.

"Barrington Bunny," one of Martin Bell's best known tales, is a Christmas story about a bunny who enjoys being furry and hopping in the snow. Sadly, Barrington was the only bunny in the forest. On Christmas Eve he was not welcome at the squirrel's party because he could not climb trees. The beavers did not welcome him because he could not swim. The field mice were having too much fun to notice him. "What good is it to be furry and to be able to hop if you don't have any family on Christmas Eve?"[2] thought Barrington.

As the bunny despaired the wolf appeared and confirmed Barrington's worth. Hopping and being furry is a special gift for the right time. "All the animals of the forest are your family,"[3] the wolf said, before disappearing. Encouraged, Barrington took a stick to give the beavers and some leaves to give the squirrels. On the way home Barrington found a baby field mouse freezing in the snow. Barrington covered him with his own warm fur all night long. In the morning the little mouse was fine, but Barrington was frozen. The wolf came, stood over Barrington's dead body all Christmas day, and disappeared.

The traditional big bad wolf eats children and is, therefore, the ultimate symbol of destruction. In the Russian story of "Peter and the Wolf," so wonderfully set to music by Sergei Prokofiev, the wolf eats the duck and threatens the children, who are finally saved by Grandfather. The wolf represents the destructive power of the forest, which in turn symbolizes the dark and unknown realities of life. The French

The silver wolf watches over Barrington Bunny

children's song *Promenon Nous* carries the same symbolism.

Promenon nous dans le bois
Pendant le lou n'est pas la
Si le lou y etais
Il nous mangerais
(Translation)
Walk the forest with delight
While the wolf is out of sight
Were the wolf already here
He would eat us without fear

The image of the wolf as a God-figure conveys not only a fearsome and awful God but one with saving grace as well as awesome and wonderful power. When children's stories simply refer to the love of God, but neglect to mention God as the source and end of life, they diminish God to a very small projection of human ideals. The Christian God of love is the one who proposes and disposes of all things in life, the alpha and omega, the beginning and the end. Perhaps because of its traditional fearsome image the wolf can be viewed as nurturing without losing the awesome qualities. Recent studies of the communal nature of the wolf pack point in that same direction.

Bell leaves little question about what he wishes to convey with the story. Barrington Bunny's perception that he is the only bunny in the forest is distorted because all of the animals are essentially one family. Barrington reflects the human propensity to be turned in upon one's self, to be lonely in the crowd, to believe that one's self or one's group is isolated. Christianity teaches that life without God is a lonely life. There is an inclination in humans to replace God with one's own ego and then to discover that one is alone. To truly sense God's presence is to be open to others. To pray genuinely is to pray as a human community. Jesus taught us to pray "Our Father" rather than "My Father."

The wolf appears with the message that all the animals of the forest are one family. While this may be true in principle, in fact, the human community often rejects one another. The evidence of care is often missing. Barrington laments that he has nothing to give to the other animals and they reject him for not being a squirrel or a beaver. All Barrington possesses is warm fur and the joy of hopping. The wolf's answer is that furriness and hopping are divine gifts. Their usefulness to others will become evident in time. As in Jesus' story of the talents, we are not to be motivated by the size of our talent, but by the willingness to invest it in others. The man with the single talent did not err by having only one talent, but by failing to invest what he had been given.So Barrington does not err in being a bunny, but in failing to invest his gifts in the lives of others.

Barrington understands the wolf's message and takes gifts of leaves to the squirrels and sticks to the beavers. Finding the lost baby field mice, he realizes that his furry body can keep them warm. The act of giving, however, costs him his life. Again the message seems quite clear. If we give with the kind of love that Christ gave to us, we should expect that we will lose our lives in the process. However, the giving of life to life is the truth of God's love. Bell vividly describes the scene in which the furry bunny's heart is near to other heartbeat of the mice, for there is the closeness of life to life.

The story is not tragic because the bunny's life was fulfilled in acts of giving. The wolf coming to stand over the dead bunny is a sign that the divine truth and love is present. The bunny's furriness and hopping have found their eternal significance in the attitude of giving.

There are several problems in this story in terms of the gospel. One is that the acts of giving seem isolated and without responsive relationships. The leaves and twigs are laid at the squirrel's and beaver's homes without acknowledgment. True, these animals discover them later, but the deeds seem all the more hidden. The parents of the field mice, as well, are unaware of who has saved the two babies. Bell is surely suggesting that giving should be in secret, so that God who sees in secret will reward the giver, a reference to the Sermon on the Mount.

This may be compared to *The Velveteen Rabbit,* who desires to become real. The velveteen rabbit learns that one becomes real when someone else really loves you. It may hurt. Your eyes may fall out and you may be roughed up, but these are all a part of becoming real. The giving of the velveteen rabbit occurs in a relationship in which, inevitably, there will be misunderstanding and hurt. Since the relational is missing in the story of Barrington Bunny, the giving still seems quite lonely.

There is no resurrection in the story of Barrington Bunny even though there are the lives of the two baby field mice, spared by Barrington's heroic action. The squirrels and beavers are also surprised. But the story ends with the impact of the dead bunny. It has the starkness of Hans Christian Andersen's *Little Match Girl,* in which the girl freezes in the snow while trying to carry out her father's orders to sell more matches. Bruno Bettleheim suggests that a fairy tale must assist a child in solving an emotional dilemma. In this story the dilemma, clearly, is that of deep loneliness. The solution is in the divine possibility of giving one's self. However, the giving is in isolation and seems to intensify the loneliness. Being a part of the family is denied to the one who gives. While the story does address inward pain, it seems never to break through to the joy that belongs to the gospel.

Bell's story about "The Porcupine Whose Name Didn't Matter" seems to come closer to the relational love and joy that belong to the gospel.[4] A porcupine who is generally gruff and hard to get along with finds an injured possum. The injury is so serious that the possum, clearly, won't live. Yet the porcupine tends the possum, without speaking much, in his usual gruff manner. Finally, the possum does die and the porcupine admits to his own insecurities and need for love. The possum obviously needed the porcupine, and the porcupine, less obviously, needed the possum. The porcupine finally acknowledges his name to the dead possum.

The important consideration is not that the name was withheld until after the possum died but that both possum and porcupine were able to give of themselves in the presence of the other's need. Both grew in that relationship. Telling his name is an indication of how much the porcupine grew. He had lost some of his gruffness and loneliness and was able finally to express it. The story is not without pain, but it has the joy and hope that is missing in "Barrington Bunny." For the porcupine and possum love is relational, an ongoing communication. The porcupine grows after the possum's death, a sign of resurrection. The "Porcupine Whose Name Doesn't Matter" seems to represent a fuller range of the gospel than does "Barrington Bunny."

Shel Silverstein's popular story, *The Giving Tree,* has some of the same limitations as "Barrington Bunny." In Silverstein's story the boy takes the tree's fruit, leaves, limbs, and wood until finally there is nothing left. In the process the boy becomes an old man. All he can do is sit on the stump of the giving tree and remember all that the tree has given him. When the tree is seen as a pattern of human behavior, everything is given without any responsiveness, just as in "Barrington Bunny." The result is a radically lonely love. If the story is seen as a human rejection of God's creation, and finally of God, then it discloses the way that human beings misuse the creation and one another. The point of the story then should be mutual respect and care, which often seems to be missed. The loneliness and the appeal to ideal giving seem to overwhelm the call to mutuality.

A contemporary writer who, like Martin Bell, wants to express the gospel in new images is Katherine Paterson. A story for which she won the coveted Newbery Children's Book Award is called *Bridge to Terabithia.*[5] It is an account of a very unusual relationship like that of the porcupine and the possum. A fifth grade boy and girl become very good friends. At an age when boys and girls will hardly speak to one another Jess, almost against his will, develops a close friendship with Leslie, whose family has moved recently to an adjoining farm in Virginia. Gradually they become inseparable friends. Their own private kingdom of friendship and imagination is a wooded area on the land where Leslie lives. They agree to call their kingdom Terabithia, and to enter it only in the proper manner by swinging on a rope over a stream. One rainy day in the spring

Jess's teacher invites him to go to visit an art gallery in Washington, DC, and he decides to go without Leslie. While he is away Leslie decides to go to Terabithia without him, but the rope breaks as she is swinging over the swollen and raging stream below. She is drowned. Jess returns from his wonderful trip to learn that his best friend is dead. In the days that follow, his emotions which range from rage to keen loss, overwhelm him. His parents and teachers attempt to support him, but Jess must learn to endure the loss. He has to come to terms with a God who would take the life of a close friend, an innocent young girl. In an act of hope Jess builds a bridge across the stream and introduces his little sister to Terabithia.

The story of this unusual friendship shows how rare and beautiful such a relationship is. It is a genuine friendship in which each gains something needful. Jess, at first, is jealous of Leslie's ability to outrun every boy in the fifth grade, but then he comes to admire her grace and intelligence. She

Jess and Leslie in Terabithia

leads him to express ideas and interests that no one else can. The pettiness of family jealousies disappear in her presence. He admires and understands her as no one else does. Her own interests and intelligence no longer seem odd in Jess's presence. The relationship enhances them both. It is not a one-way relationship of lonely giving, but a genuine interaction. Jealousy and timidity are overcome by admiration, encouragement, and free-flowing imagination. It expresses the wonder, beauty, and joy of a mutual relationship which is at the same time always fragile.

The relationship of Jess and Leslie is reminiscent of the Apostle Paul's description of the church as a communion of persons in which the gift of each is needed to fulfill the community. God's providence is such that various gifts have been distributed among persons, and each of these gifts fulfills the other. To be in Christ is not to consider one gift more important than another, but to contribute so that the body of Christ may function well and that Christ is exalted in the process. Christian love is a mutual fulfillment of one another in the midst of the jealousies and difficulties that inevitably arise. One cannot expect or demand that such friendship occur. One can only be thankful when it is given because true mutual friendship is a mark of God's grace.

Paterson writes about the real difficulties children experience. Where actual pain is not realized, there can be no hope or encouragement. The difficulties of adulthood are, to a very large extent, the extension of the joy and pain of childhood. Stories that touch the genuine experiences of children offer the greatest source of hope. Children in the twentieth century face abuse, brutality, starvation, and atomic threat. Few persons have an innocent and unscarred childhood. Yet the desire to protect children from the pain of life may lead to attempting to surround children with a kind of false security that seeks to insulate them from pain. The result can be that their actual pain is never understood and must be borne without help.

All children experience death, and many experience it in the death of a close friend or member of the family. Paterson's story about Jess and Leslie helps children live through this experience realistically, yet with hope. Jess wants to blot out the awful, painful loss that he feels. Angry at others and at God as well, he tries to run from reality. He sees the awkardness and poverty in other people's response. Taunted by other children, he yet discovers how much others loved Leslie, and is joined to them in a new and surprising way.

Bridge to Terebithia explores a child's response to the reality of death, something that children need. Indeed, it is something that everyone needs. The reality of death is accepted, and the enduring word is acknowledged. New possibilities and new relationships spring up from the pain in surprising ways. Paterson is true to the gospel without constantly making a point of it. In Jess's experience one can see the disciples' experience in response to the death of Jesus as well as how resurrection comes as new hope. Paterson lets the gospel story influence the contemporary story.

Perhaps the story of Jess and Leslie is so powerful because Paterson's own son experienced the death of a close friend, a girl. It happened when they were both only seven, and the enduring loss of that experience motivated the author to write a fictional account that would deal with the reality of death for children. To accept the reality of death is part of the depth of life, and to sense the victory of hope over death is the center of the gospel message. Persons of all ages need this story. Children do not need it in terms of a religious confession which belongs better in later years. They need, rather, to have their own pain touched with hope. One learns from *Bridge to Terabithia* that while there is little to do in the face of tragedy and pain, one can begin to face that reality and to trust that new possibilities will arise. God's love is always deeper than our despair.

The process of reforming the wolf is constantly ongoing. The wolf represents our fears, which at base are rooted in the anxiety of morality. That the awesome wolf can be nurturant and caring is at first unbelievable. Yet the one who does not know the awesomeness of God cannot plumb God's love.

Notes

1. Martin Bell, *The Way of the Wolf,* (New York: Ballentine Books, 1970), p. 5.
2. Bell, *The Way of the Wolf,* p. 5.
3. Bell, *The Way of the Wolf,* p. 6.
4. Bell, *The Way of the Wolf,* pp. 111-119.
5. Katherine Paterson, *Bridge to Terabitha,* (New York: Avon Books, 1978).

·11·

The Power of Christ

"It means," said Aslan, "that though the Witch knew the Deep Magic, there is a magic deeper still which she did not know."[1]

The Narnia tales are C. S. Lewis's attempt to symbolize the truth of the gospel for youth in a very direct way. In a sense they are in the tradition of *Pilgrim's Progress*, although they do not represent Puritan theology. The wonderful imagination of the Narnia tales have made them very popular with children. As much as any of the stories referred to in this book, they attempt through a fictional narrative to give a full and fundamental account of the Christian gospel.

Perhaps the best known of the Narnia series is the first, *The Lion, the Witch and the Wardrobe*. It is the story of four children, Lucy, Susan, Peter, and Edmund who discover an entry into another land through the back of an old professor's wardrobe. In their first visit they discover that Narnia is a land of perpetual snow ruled over by a wicked queen. Those who oppose the will of the queen are turned to stone to adorn her palace.

In the next visit to Narnia, Edmund is captured by the queen, who entrances him with "Turkish delight," a food that is wonderfully delicious; however, the more one eats, the more one wants. The other children escape capture through the help of friendly animals. They find that their only hope of final release is Aslan, a great lion who is more powerful than the witch. They race to where Aslan is expected, only to find that the queen is already there. The queen threatens to kill Edmund unless

Aslan submits to her wishes. In order to save Edmund, Aslan allows himself to be placed on a great stone tablet, shorn of his mane and killed. The witch had thought that a life can be saved only by the giving of a life. She was not aware that a life freely given for another breaks the grip of death and evil. Aslan's resurrection initiates a battle between the forces of Aslan and of the witch, whose forces are now hopelessly overpowered. Aslan takes the children on his back to the witch's palace, where he touches all the frozen animals, who immediately return to life. The forces of the witch defeated, the children are placed on thrones to rule over the land.

The struggle of good and evil is central to the story. For inexplicable reasons some persons are more inclined to evil than others. Edmund is grumpier, more difficult to get along with, and more susceptible to the charms of the witch. So it is he who falls prey to the witch and who betrays the presence

Lucy, Susan, Peter and Edmund through the wardrobe

of the others. It is finally Edmund for whom Aslan has to give his own life. One cannot explain why there are those persons who are more susceptible to temptation. It may be a matter of disposition, circumstance, or choice, but finally there is a mystery to it. Theology has always directed itself to God's mysterious creative will in pondering why some are more open to temptation. Circumstance and choice are not sufficient explanations in themselves. On the other hand, circumstance and choice explain in large measure how temptation occurs.

The witch represents the drawing power of will. She is enormously attractive, beautiful to behold, but her touch leaves one frozen forever. Whatever she rules becomes freezing cold. Evil is usually portrayed as attractive. Even when evil is ugly, there is something captivating about it too. The witch appeared to be the ideal of beauty, and offered a food that was irresistible. However, the food only increased one's appetite and the beauty was cold and unapproachable. Evil is beauty without nurturance. Beneath the beauty lies anger and destructiveness. The witch's satisfaction comes from having persons under her destructive control which, finally, becomes the power of her own self-destruction.

Why does Lewis portray evil as feminine? Does this illustrate an anti-feminine bias in the story? Evil is usually depicted as masculine, as rebellious disobedience. The biblical stories nearly always show evil as a temptation as in Eden where the snake tempted Adam and Eve with the fruit of knowledge. Jacob wrestled all night with the angel at Peniel. David was tempted by the sight of Bathsheba. Jesus was tempted in the desert at Caesarea Philippi and again at Gethsemane. Evil is a temptation.

Lewis portrays evil as a temptress, and it is Edmund and not Lucy who succumbs. The Christian tradition has so often stressed the weakness of women and the fall of woman as the means of the fall of man. Lewis's account has the boy yielding to temptation. Perhaps Lewis is influenced by his own experience. While at boarding school in his early teens, he had a sexual relationship with an older woman. The experience was so fraught with guilt for him that it led to

The queen watches Aslan being shorn of his mane

losing his faith. Lewis's teenage sexual experience, that lack of satisfying relationship, and the ensuing destructive guilt may explain the story of Edmund's fall.

The story seems especially true to the male experience of temptation and fall. It is not so sensitive to the female experience. Evil may be intelligence and beauty without compassion and love. Evil surely is intelligence covering self-destructive control and can be both feminine and masculine. Lewis's symbol of the witch makes it seem especially feminine while the masculine image, Aslan, is a symbol of goodness. The result is that the relation of masculine and feminine to evil is weighted in the feminine direction. For some persons the use of the witch as symbol may be valid, but it should be balanced with other narratives.

Lewis's account of evil as lack of love is very biblical. A world without love is a frozen world. The evil witch always brings beautiful snow and severe cold. The other tradition is that evil is accompanied by chaotic emotion and burning conflict. Both may be true. Evil can, at times, be chaotic conflict and, at other times, loveless control. For that matter the two can exist at the same time. Love can overcome conflict and bring care back to control.

Lewis's picture of the evil witch set the stage for the appearance of Aslan and goodness. The lion is a symbol of great strength, and in the story, of great nurturance. The children feel protected even by the hope of Aslan's coming which overcomes the certainty of being eternally frozen in the witch's court yard. It is the hope of life and joy. The story of Aslan's coming is good news for all those who have only the snowy wilderness to anticipate.

The heart of the gospel is revealed in Aslan's giving of himself for Edmund. Life is so ordered by God that one life can be released only by the sacrifice of another. Lewis portrays creation as governed by life living off of other life. The sacrificial character of living is written into the nature of things. This gives evil its power. The desire of everyone to save one's own life allows evil to reign. When one freely gives one's life for the sake of another, the power of evil is broken.

Thus Lewis portrays Christ's sacrifice for sin. Christ satisfied the requirement of life for life, but Christ's freely giving his life broke the power of evil. The law of Moses was fulfilled and at the same time transcended. The struggle of good and evil continues, but now the victory of love is certain. When the risen Christ comes, the power of good over evil will be complete. Those who were frozen by evil will come alive in the warmth of God's love.

Another Christian writer of children's stories is Madeleine L'Engle. Like Lewis she uses her writing to give new symbols to old images. Her book, *Wrinkle In Time,* winner of the 1963 Newbery book award, is for older children and teens.[2] She wrestles directly, but not obviously, with central issues in the Christian message. The story takes place on another planet in outer space, touching the contemporary imagination. In this book females are not subordinate to the males, and so, again, it is close to the modern experience.

The story is about several children whose father has disappeared. From Mrs. Who, How, and Why they discover that he has been taken to another planet. They also discover how to *tesseract* to other times and spaces which is done by passing through a "wrinkle in time." Quickly they go to search for their father.

On the other planet the children find a population in total conformity, with everything being done according to schedule and in the prescribed manner. This is a controlled society, one without emotion and individual interest. The children also discover that their father has been walled into a transparent cylinder, visible, but imprisoned. There seems to be no way to reach him.

Finally they discover that the society is governed by "the thing," a human brain without emotion. It keeps everything running in perfect order, but without feelings and love. The children find that they hate "the thing," and that they are absolutely powerless in its presence. There seems to be no hope of freeing their father.

However, for one moment Susan feels just a glimmer of compassion for "the thing" and in that moment discovers that its power is diminished. Armed with this knowledge and the small ray of compassion, the children return to their imprisoned father where Susan is able to penetrate the cylinder to join him. When they are reunited the cylinder loses its strength and they are able to leave.

It is when they *tesseract* back through time and space to Earth that they arrive at still a third planet where they find a group of "beasts" who live by feeling rather than sight, by emotion rather than technical order. Though the "beasts" cannot see, they can sense how others feel. They give support and nurture to one another, and to their visitors. The children and their father find themselves wonderfully welcomed and cared for in the land of the "beasts."

When the children and their father finally return to Earth they gain a new vision of Earth as they approach. They find Earth caught in a tremendous struggle between the two worlds where they have been. In many ways Earth is headed toward domination by "the thing," but the world is also drawn to the community of the "beasts." Earth is caught in the struggle with the outcome still undecided.

Madeleine L'Engle uses the device of two other worlds to portray the evil and good tendencies of human society. Evil is depicted as loveless intelligence, as a totally computer-oriented society where structure is all important. Earlier we noted that evil has classically been portrayed as lack of wisdom, rebellion, or compassion. L'Engle is strongly on the side of lack of compassion.

The one possibility of overcoming the power of "the thing" is the smallest feeling of compassion for the situation of another creature. "The thing" objectifies all reality. All things become objects for manipulation. The one possibility of breaking the constraints of objectivity is a moment of subjectivity. Love joins two creatures in their subjectivity. They become centers of freedom for one another.

L'Engle's vision of evil is more subjective than C.S. Lewis's who considers evil to be the power of an eye for an eye and a tooth for a tooth. For every life another life must be paid. Evil is appetite without deeper wisdom. The witch is clever but she is beautiful and willful. "The thing" is primarily intelligence and, certainly, ugly. Evil is very unattractive in L'Engle's vision, but almost impossible to resist.

In Lewis's account evil can be touched only by an act that satisfies the law of selfishness. The giving of a life is required, but, voluntarily given, it overcomes evil. In L'Engle's account a moment of love must enter in. Christ's giving of himself is a sense of compassion for those who kill him. That moment of compassion changes the course of history.

Evil is more feminine in character for Lewis and more masculine for L'Engle. The attractive power of evil is clearly feminine in the person of the witch. Evil is more neutral in "the thing," but orderly intelligence is closer to the traditional male image.

The two visions of evil are within the same tradition even though contrasts can be pointed out. Evil is an imprisonment because of a fundamental selfishness. That imprisonment is almost totally irresistible without the presence of a saving power that turns persons away from themselves and toward one another. Both stories in their own way point to the power of Christ.

The description of goodness is already implicit in what has been said. The goodness of Aslan is his power to give his own life to break the witch's power. Aslan knows what the witch does not know, that a life voluntarily given will break the law of life for life. The deeper knowledge affects the will of all who experience release through Aslan. Goodness is the renewal of life that comes from the power of God through the death and resurrectionof Christ. It is objectivity given to those who know and trust its power.

In Madeleine L'Engle's account goodness is the basic love and compassion for other beings that sustain the creation. Without this love all things may be in an orderly structure but it may be basically destructive to the human spirit. The spirit of love is not easily attained. It comes as a surprise almost in spite of one's self and it may require great self-sacrifice.

Just as compassion for "thing" came to the children, light of a changed feeling and perspective. Christ's life is the presence in history of such a changed perspective. In the cross one sees the depth of Christ's compassion for those who crucified him. In doing so they were following a system of justice, one that aspired to noble goals, but did so without love. Law without love and compassion becomes evil. Under this kind of law all persons become objects and come under the power of death. The love of Christ breaks the power of death.

Lewis's account stresses the more objective side of the power of Christ. He shows how certain structures of reality have been created and govern all things. Evil has knowledge of those structures, but an insufficient knowledge. The perversion of will and loss of compassion follow evil.

L'Engle's story stresses the more subjective side of the power of Christ. Love comes through human feeling and imagination affect perception and will. One begins to feel differently toward the very power of evil in its immediate presence. Love gives rise to love. The power of evil lovelessness is broken. The stress is upon the human response of love to love. Everyone, collectively and individually, is in the struggle to decide whether to respond in compassionate ways, or whether to respond, perhaps intelligently, but without compassion.

The "beasts" represent the kingdom of God. They do not judge outward appearances, but according to the depths of the soul. They nourish and sustain everyone who comes into contact with them. They represent the ultimate power of goodness that will finally prevail in life. Their caring makes them vulnerable and they may suffer from those who objectify all of life, but their way is finally the truer way. In the meantime all are caught in the struggle of response.

A more subjective definition of love is that it must be a deep personal expression. Lewis's more objective description indicates that love must express the deep structures of creation. The one definition expresses personal conviction and expression and the other, reality and certainty. Christianity through the years has defined the power of Christ's love in both ways. In fact, both are needed to plumb the depths of Christ's love and they are complementary. God's love in Christ is both the assurance that sin has been overcome and the actual personal embodiment of love in the lives of responsive people.

Stories like *The Lion, The Witch and The Wardrobe,* and *A Wrinkle In Time* give new imaginative expression to aspects of the gospel. They do it in such a way that children can understand. With power of fascinating narrative, they do not simply repeat the gospel story, but recreate it in a new way. Each reader is encouraged to make the story a part of the narrative of the reader's life. Being a Christian is more a matter of writing a new narrative based upon the pattern of the gospel than it is the application of certain principles. Stories like that of C. S. Lewis and Madeleine L'Engle can help readers to anticipate their own stories. But that has always been the function of story. The storyteller creates the reality in which people live.

Notes

1. C. S. Lewis, *The Lion, The Witch, and The Wardrobe,* (New York: The Macmillan Company, 1960).
2. Madeleine L'Engle, *A Wrinkle in Time.* (New York: Farrar, Straus & Giroux, Inc., 1962).

Epilogue

The essays in this book have been an effort to view selected examples of classical children's stories from the perspective of the gospel. The gospel is the good news that the God who created us is also present with us in Jesus Christ reclaiming and reconciling us to God and to one another. The story of the life, death, and resurrection of Jesus the Christ has the power to turn all our stories into hopeful stories, no matter how discouraging or tragic they may seem to be. "God was in Christ reconciling the world to God" becomes the focal point and the frame of reference of all our individual stories as well as of our national stories and of all human history.

Since Jesus Christ is the name above all names, the power beyond all powers, the story of Jesus is also the story beyond all stories. The story of Jesus reconciles all other stories to God's intention. God also gives a wider framework for all other stories. It is therefore possible to view children's stories within the framework of the gospel. In doing so one does not change the child's story nor supplant it; rather one enters into a conversation between the gospel and the story. One of the characteristics of the gospel is to affirm every story in its own terms. So the inward power and beauty of a story is enhanced in the perspective of the gospel; the deficiency and ugliness of a story may also become evident and reconciled within the gospel story.

Recalling some of the comparisons of these essays will help to focus their central point. The historical significance of the Mother Goose stories derives from their power to

They represent a collection of a wide variety of genres including puzzles, finger plays, fables, historical episodes, word plays, and nonsense syllables. The simple charm of the poetry defies any effort to find real meaning. Yet they are one with the gospel in affirming the wonder and variety of life and language.

One may play with a poem like "Peter, Peter, Pumpkin Eater" and wonder about the significance of keeping a wife, pumpkin eating, and learning. Without knowing exactly the significance of the words, one may note that the gospel encourages a mutuality between husband and wife. Christianity has also been a good soil in which education has grown. Should pumpkin eating be a symbol of poverty, one may note that the gospel is concerned that people be released from poverty.

Are the Mother Goose stories too full of violence or too prone to stereotype the gender roles of boys and girls? Such questions are worthy of the gospel, for the gospel addresses violence and oppression between human beings. One cannot tell the story of the crucifixion without some reference to violence, nor can one tell of Jesus' relationship with women without challenging gender stereotyping. To remove all references to violence is to remove stories from life the way it actually is. Such sanitized stories will be powerless for children in the long run. But dwelling on violence, or describing it outside the context of hope and love can injure the hearer. The violence of the gospel is described within the context of the love of God and is, therefore, history's greatest source of hope. The humor of much Mother Goose violence can speak to the deep fears of children, especially when the story offers a hopeful solution and when the storyteller is one who loves the child.

In the same way, to remove all stories that have stereotyped roles of boys and girls would be unrealistic. Those stories carry the history of the human race in a way that small children can understand. But a diet of stories of only aggressive boys and passive girls is out of touch with the freedom called for in the gospel. Children need stories free of the older gender stereotyping.

Turning from the Mother Goose stories to folktales, one cannot help wondering whether the stories collected by the Brothers Grimm are not terribly out of date. Yet such an astute observer as poet W. H. Auden considers these tales along with the Bible as the twin foundations of Western Culture. The psychologist, Bruno Bettelheim, has also argued for folktales as essential to the emotional health of children. Folktales very often give a solution to an emotional problem that very many children have. The story speaks indirectly, while more direct advice from a parent or teacher would be resisted by the child.

The theme of Hansel and Gretel is hunger. The story describes what happens to persons who are dominated by the urge to eat. Only when Hansel and Gretel are able to restrain their appetites are they able to escape the witch and return to their father. Similarly the gospel is concerned about being dominated by appetites. As Israel constrains its appetite in the wilderness, it gains God's guidance; and as Christ constrains his appetite in the wilderness, he gains the power of the Messiah. The limiting of appetite is central to the gospel story, but it comes not simply from an exercise of intelligence or will. Rather, freedom comes from the grace of God, and then all our relationships are changed. The story of Hansel and Gretel touches a very fundamental gospel theme, but without reference to God. The folktale has very great power, as is attested by hundreds of years of telling the story. It need not be changed. It helps illuminate the gospel as the gospel deepens its significance.

As was previously mentioned, to eliminate Hansel and Gretel because it refers to bad stepmothers, witches, and eating children is a serious mistake. The story speaks to such feelings and symbols in an indirect way, and in a way by which those feelings are to be resolved. For most children the story is helpful rather than harmful. It also helps us to tell the gospel story which is often too sanitized for young children. If we love to eat more than we love God and one another, we will become very greedy persons.

In the stories of Hans Christian Anderson are to be found many themes, such as simplicity, integrity, compassion and enjoyment of the present. Anderson is considered to be a Romantic because he could evoke the depths of feeling in any situation by his simple descriptions. The story of the ugly duckling brings out sympathy for the one who is misunderstood and ridiculed by nearly everyone nearby. It calls for a kind of faith in oneself until one's inward strength and grace is revealed.

The gospel knows what it is to be misunderstood. "Blessed are you when men revile you and persecute you and utter all kinds of evil against you falsely on my account." (Matt. 5:11) The deeper joy of life will come in spite of persecution.

Hans Christian Anderson seems to know something of waiting and hoping in time of persecution, for the story of the ugly duckling describes it well. Possibly Anderson is too passive in his waiting, and possibly the hope does not name God. Yet the gospel story makes clear that Anderson's waiting is very much like faith, and Anderson's story illuminates what it means to be persecuted for righteousness sake. All of this is done in a story that touches the heart of almost every child. We would not change Anderson's story, but it does need other stories to complement it, stories of those who are not so passive as the ugly duckling.

Each storyteller brings out a different facet of the gospel, one that might otherwise go unnoticed. Contrast the poetry of Robert Louis Stevenson and the stories of A. A. Milne in the light of the gospel. Stevenson always seems to stand on the edge of forever. His poetry has a way of taking common, everyday experiences and finding them filled with the beyond. The rain that is raining on you and me is also raining on the ships at sea. The cupful of water that rises in a small hole dug by a child in the sand is the same water that fills the sea. So the coincidence of the immediate and of eternity is always present in Stevenson's poetry.

Milne is concerned about other things. His raindrops race one another to the bottom of the window pane. The boy who steps on the squares is relating to the bears. Christopher Robin's friends are always getting into impossible situations with one another. Milne seems concerned about how persons must learn to adapt to differences of character if community is to be possible. Of course there are many other themes also, but the theme of differences within community seems to be central.

Comparison of the stories of each story teller evokes a different feature of the gospel. Stevenson reminds us that the gospel is the story of God's presence in the everyday occurrences of life. Milne reminds us that the gospel is the story of how very different persons are bound together in a common body by Christ's love. Both of these themes are essential to the gospel. We do not need to change Stevenson's poetry or Milne's stories to find gospel parallels.

Lewis Carroll and Frank Baum speak of other worlds in very different ways. Lewis Carroll's Wonderland is a land of embarrassment, rudeness, and threatened violence. "Off with their heads," cries the queen upon any provocation. Alice moves through Wonderland with relative innocence, courtesy, and constantly seeking meaning among a myriad of nonsensical paradoxes. Only when Alice protests the injustice and reminds herself that after all, it is only a dream, only then does Wonderland disappear.

Frank Baum's Oz is also a land of threatening violence. However, Dorothy and her friends are able to solve problems in Oz that Alice can never solve in Wonderland. Dorothy does manage to find the Wizard, defeat the wicked witch of the West, find courage, wisdom, and sympathy for her friends, and discover the secret of returning home. There were answers and she could do something about it. For Alice there was no answer to the puzzle, "How is a raven like a writing desk?" Alice never seems to be going anywhere, and she gets home simply by remembering that it is all a dream.

The world of Lewis Carroll is full of meaninglessness. Childlike virtue and courtesy allows one what hope there is. The world of Frank Baum has solutions, but they are to be found within oneself. No one can give you courage or wisdom; they are already yours. The gospel portrays the world as fallen and meaningless outside God's love, somewhat like Wonderland. Under God's love the world has purpose and direction, somewhat like Oz. The way through the world is to receive God's grace and live in the power of God's love. Joy comes as both an act of will (Alice) and of intelligence (Dorothy), but primarily as the presence of God's grace. Like Dorothy's courage, sympathy, and wisdom, the Kingdom of God is found to be already among us.

The stories of Uncle Remus show how an oppressed people can survive in their weakness. If Brer Rabbit cannot dominate Brer Fox, he can outsmart him. The gospel is also the story of release from oppression. We are to remember that at one time we were no people, counted as nobodies in the world. Then Christ redeemed us with his own life and blood. Now we who were no one are precious in God's sight. So we are to consider everyone precious in our sight. The power of Christ is the power of weakness, the power of the meek to inherit the earth. To be Christlike is to love one's enemies and to do good to those who do evil to you. The power of weakness is not simply the power of being wiser, although that is not inappropriate; it is living in the power of Christ. We need not change Uncle Remus's stories to let them show that the gospel story is a story of liberation.

Martin Bell's *Way of the Wolf* intends to speak of God. To find parallels to the gospel in no way stretches the stories, for they are meant to be the gospel in new images. The wolf is a powerful, wonderful presence that gives courage to all the animals. The wolf combines awesome power, cunning and great gentleness, so symbolizing God's fundamental characteristics. The presence of the wolf leads the animals to service, care, and the touching of life and life.

C. S. Lewis's Narnia tales also intend to speak of the gospel. They show a world that is frozen when dominated by cold, uncaring beauty and appetite. Only the willingness of Aslan to be humiliated and killed releases the animals and people from the power of their own self-serving appetites. With Aslan's power the children are able to reign in the new kingdom. Aslan points directly to the love of Christ releasing people from sin so that they might reign in God's Kingdom. Lewis's story fascinates children and at the same time gives contemporary form to the gospel story.

The point of these essays is that the gospel has the power to focus and deepen any story. The gospel also shows the inadequacies, perhaps the ugliness of a story, but in such a way as to point to God's reconciliation in Jesus Christ. All stories can be seen in the light of the gospel, and therefore, so can children's stories. My call is not to convert children, but to let their lives be surrounded by the love of Christ. As Christ becomes the center of a community's life, the stories they tell will be drawn into conversation with the story of Christ.

May parents and teachers be more concerned to tell stories to children, for in such stories children gain the symbols by which they interpret reality. The rich heritage of children's stories need not be changed unless indeed they dwell on violence, hopelessness, or cynicism. However the storyteller ought to be aware of how the story does or does not reflect the gospel. Since the gospel is endlessly reflective, the essays here simply begin the discussion rather than end it. The story media of this age, of which television is perhaps the foremost, ought to be considered in view of what is being taught. Perhaps teachers and parents can be encouraged to reclaim story telling.

Children need a rich array of stories, and they need a community of storytellers who care about them. The great wealth of stories available to children gives the interested adult so many possibilities to relate to children. The community of faith will always have the gospel story in mind, no matter what story is being told. So the community of faith will learn to tell the gospel story in many new ways, which fits the intention of the gospel. Alongside the many stories being told, the gospel story is also to be told in many ways. The conversation between the gospel and the many stories will enrich those stories and will let the gospel story illuminate all of life.

Suggestions for Further Reading

For the reader who wants to look further, the wealth of materials on the meaning of children's stories is overwhelming.

A survey of children's literature is a good place to begin. One of the best is Zena Sutherland and May Hill Arbuthnot, *Children and Books* (Glencoe, IL: Scott Foresman and Company, 1985), which gives the whole range of children's literature and illustrations.

A resource that discusses the religious values of children's literature is *Children's Literature for all God's Children* by Virginia Coffin Thomas and Betty Davis Miller (Atlanta: John Knox Press, 1986). They suggest 194 stories for children along with evaluative comment and include many resources as well as a list of children's book awards.

Another book that explores the place of children's literature in religious education is Gladys Hunt's *Honey for a Child's Heart* (Grand Rapids, MI: Zondervan Publishing House, 1978). After many suggestions about choosing books for children, Hunt offers a bibliography of several hundred stories categorized roughly according to preschool, middlers, and teens. She is especially interested in religious stories.

Nancy Larrick's *A Parent's Guide to Children's Reading* (Philadelphia: Westminister Press, 1982) has many suggestions for enlarging children's interest in reading. She has an annotated bibliography of perhaps 1000 stories for children as well as a list of books and magazines about children's reading.

A wonderful but expensive source of stories is Sharon Sprodemann Dreyer, *The Bookfinder: A Guide to Children's Literature about the Needs and Problems of Youth Aged 2-15,* 2 vols (Circle Pines, MN: American Guidance Service, 1977, 1981). The *Bookfinder* organizes the book according to 450 topics such as values, self-esteem, family conflict, and so forth. A summary is given for each book listed.

John T. Gillespie and Christine B. Gilbert, eds., *Best Books for Children,* 2nd ed. (New York: R. K. Bowker, 1981) has a list of 13,000 titles. The books are arranged according to subject and each story is summarized.

Another fine but very expensive resource is Dolores Blythe Jones, *Children's Literature Awards and Winners. A Directory of Prizes, Authors, and Illustrators,* 1st ed. (Detroit: Neal-Schuman and Gale Research Co., 1983). Titles of award winning books are given. This book may be found in a public library reference collection.

Katherine Patterson's *Gates of Excellence: On Reading and Writing Books for Children* (New York: Elsovier/Nelson, 1981) discusses the quality of writing for children. Because of the excellence of her own writing for children, her comments are quite interesting.

Rebecca J. Lukens, *A Critical Handbook of Children's Literature,* 2nd. ed. (Glenville, IL: Scott Foresman, 1982) explores children's literature according to adult criteria for genre, character, plot, setting, point of view, style, tone, and theme. It therefore has some similarity to this present work.

Mary Ann Paulsen, *Creative Uses of Children's Literature* (Hamden, CT: Library Professional Publication, 1982) has a fine bibliography and a wealth of suggestions, many of which are appropriate to religious education.

A small book that is especially relevant to religious education is Patricia Pearl, *Religious Books for Children: An Annotated Bibliography* (Bryn Mawr, PA: Church and Synagogue Library Association, 1983). Books are arranged according to religious topics.

Mary Lou White, *Children's Literature: Criticism and Response* (Columbus, OH: Charles E. Merrill, 1976) has essays on evaluating children's literature psychologically, sociologically, structurally, and archetypically. These essays make an interesting contrast to the material in this book.

Fredrick Buechner, *Telling the Truth: The Gospel As Tragedy, Comedy, and Fairy Tale* (New York: Harper & Row, 1977) compares the gospel to classical literary genres. The dialogical approach is similar to that of the present work.

Bruno Bettelheim has shown how important stories are in the normal development of children. His book is entitled *The Uses of Enchantment: The Meaning and Importance of Fairy Tales* (New York: Alfred A. Knopf, 1976).

A book that has influenced this author very much is Roger Sale, *Fairy Tales and After, from Snow White to E. B. White* (Cambridge, MA: Harvard University Press, 1978). Sale has written a series of critical essays on famous children's stories. His comments are always provocative.

A number of lists of children's books are published, some of them periodically. For example, Mary Lou White has edited *Adventuring with Books* with more than 2500 annotated titles published by the National Council of Teachers of English, 1111 Kenyon Road, Urbana, IL 61801, 1981.

The *Caldecott Medal Books* honor outstanding illustrators and the *Newberry Medal Books* honor outstanding stories. Pamphlets listing these awards are published annually by the Association for Library Service to Children, 50 E. Huron Street, Chicago, IL 60611.

Several outstanding magazines review children's literature. One of the best, *The Horn Book,* is published bimonthly and may be ordered from The Horn Book, Park Square Building, 31 St. James Ave., Boston, MA 02116.

These suggestions are only a few in a field of rich and diverse resources. The inquiring reader will be able to find many more by following these leads.